MONEY FOR GOOD

Franklin
White

MONEY FOR
GOOD

A STREBOR BOOKS INTERNATIONAL LLC PUBLICATION
DISTRIBUTED BY SIMON & SCHUSTER, INC.

Published by

Strebor Books International LLC
P.O. Box 6505
Largo, MD 20792
http://www.streborbooks.com

ISBN 978-1-59309-040-1
LCCN 2003105029

Distributed by Simon & Schuster, Inc.
1230 Avenue of the Americas
New York, NY 10020
1-800-223-2336

Cover design: www.mariondesigns.com

First Printing November 2003
Manufactured and Printed in the United States

10 9 8 7 6 5 4 3 2

FOR

Ann E. Griffin
Carl White Sr.
Cassandra M. (Sandi) Graves
and, of course,
Marva

1

"I've been in this business a long time. And it's been my experience, as a prosecutor, that when this large amount of money is missing: the accused is a drug pusher or has a serious drug problem as well. Are you a drug addict?" the district attorney pried.

"No," answered the defendant. "What kind of question is that?"

"It's a very relevant question. A question that deserves a truthful answer."

"I did answer truthfully. Didn't you hear me? If you didn't—maybe you're the one on drugs."

I was one of eleven people serving on grand jury duty that Friday in the Federal Building on the thirteenth floor, in downtown Atlanta. Most of the lame bastards fulfilling their moral obligation with me were actually enjoying themselves—listening to the duel between the prosecutor and defendant. But hell no, I wasn't. I had things to do and money to make in my auto repair shop.

WEST OWENS DO U RIGHT
AUTO REPAIR SERVICE

I admit, my shop sign cost a mint but I had to have it after I went down to the print shop and saw over the computer screen how they could make a sign that would puff a brother up. It was nothing but a multicolored fifteen-by-fifteen-foot sign that was centered in between two wooden poles that were anchored down on the rooftop of my shop—but to me it was definitely fly. And well worth the thirty-five hundred I paid for it. It was colorful, eye-catching and made my place seem like success was sitting up in the hood.

It took me a while to decide on whether to buy it or not, but when I finally decided to plop down the cash for it, it made a nigga feel good. Not only could I see my name in the sky from two blocks away, it even laid the false pretense to the ladies on my block—one in particular; Denise, who everyone called D (who I would have done in a heartbeat if I wasn't living with my girl), that I was getting paid. But the truth of the matter was, I wasn't. A brother was flat out broke and damn near at the end of all the freaking resources I had saved the past ten years—working at Goodyear to get the shop operational.

It was a shame that I had only been open for business three weeks before I was summoned to serve. Because I was my shop's one and only employee, that meant closing up shop, wiping down the bay and putting my metal out-to-lunch sign that dangled way too much to the right, on the front door—without saying a word to anyone, as to when the hell I would be back— because I really didn't know.

Every second of all the judicial bullshit I was forced to sit and listen to—was just that—bull. Time was of the essence and my money was being compromised every minute I was away from my shop. To me, the whole process of sitting on grand jury duty was a damn joke anyway. Asking questions and expecting a muthafucka to be totally honest just because they actually raise their hand in front of a group of people they couldn't give a good sweaty fuck about. Besides, civic duty had never been my bag. Anything to do with jail, cops or lawyers had always made this black man lose his appetite. Thank God, it was late afternoon and we were hearing our last case.

"Where's the money, Rossi?" District Attorney Brent Anderson blasted away at the white boy sitting before the jury. As he answered I looked down at my watch; Anderson had been asking the same question going on fifty minutes. But this cat Pete Rossi was cooler than the air conditioning blasting the jury room. He had been ice cold since he first sat down in front of us. When he spoke, everything about him was calm and carefree. Over and over, Rossi told the DA that he didn't know where the money was, but the DA continued to press him anyway as though his life depended on it.

After a while, it was clear to me that DA Anderson couldn't hide the stress of dealing with Rossi; his jawbones were pushing, nearing a breaking point on the side of his face. There was no question that the DA wanted this guy bad. Anderson even told the jury so before Rossi strolled into the room, took off his fly (nice) suit jacket and arrogantly sat down in complete control despite the charges they had on him. I thought Anderson's speech about Rossi being a low-life and scum before we even had a chance to hear Rossi's side of the story was a bit biased. But I wasn't going to dispute the district attorney's claims. If that's how the DA wanted to present Rossi to us then the hell with it; I was ready to grant Anderson his wish and give him the guy rolled into a packed blunt so he could take Rossi to trial and smoke him. Then just maybe, I could jump in my car and get the hell on my way so I could open my shop and make my paper.

From the beginning, it wasn't long after the DA first started in with his questions that I got the feeling he didn't care too much for Rossi. For some reason *payback*, *vendetta*, even *get back*, was in the air and I couldn't figure out why. Then again, the DA didn't show too much respect for any of the defendants who appeared before the grand jury to plead their situation during the week. Anderson was a straight-up idiot who tried intimidation and the weight of his position to get what he wanted. At the outset of questioning, I thought the DA's ignorant attitude against Rossi was because Rossi had movie star qualities and had the surprising mannerisms of a black man. He was jazzy, his voice and tempo like he'd spent time in the hood with a bunch of roughneck brothers—sipping yack and passing blunts.

Rossi was a dude who had shit working for him and it didn't matter to me that he was white; I compliment when it's due. When Rossi sashayed into our presence, a few of the ladies on the jury gave each other the eye. *Eye candy* and they all wanted a piece. Compared to the DA Rossi was *god*.

He looked to be in his thirties but over thirty-five. His full head of black hair was cut perfect in one of those European styles. His teeth just had to be bleached. Rossi looked like he worked out six days a week, ate steamed broccoli on the regular and wore clothes out of *GQ*.

In the other corner, DA Anderson was a scrawny guy who stood about five-three, one thirty-five tops, with a big ass mouth and wore his suits two sizes too big. Matter of fact, Anderson wore what looked to be the same suit every day. I have to admit he didn't take any shit though. He was pissed at Rossi for fucking with him, too. Every question he asked, Rossi countered with the greatest of ease. Their back and forth was getting tiring so I started to scribble on the note pad the clerk had passed out to all the jurors. But even still as they rumbled, I couldn't entirely tune them out.

"Where's the money?" Anderson wanted to know again.

"I told you. I don't know," Rossi answered.

Anderson looked at the grand jury and shook his head in disgust. "Well, Mr. Rossi—tell us what you do know? Tell us what happened the night the money disappeared?"

Rossi took his turn to look around at us. He wasn't desperate but he tried his best to convey he was being railroaded. "There's nothing different. It's like I told you, man…and just like you've read in my statement. Bean called my cell phone minutes before I parked my car to meet him with the money and he told me to leave the money in the car but to carry my money-bag to the drop-off spot, as though everything was normal. When I asked him why, he told me not to worry because someone would pull it from under my car seat later. Now, c'mon… How many times do I have to tell you? Didn't you read your transcript counselor or listen to the tapes? It's not like I wasn't wired when this whole thing went down."

Anderson snapped back in a forced baritone pitch, "We know you were wired, Rossi."

"Just making sure."

"They know and the jury's aware that the wire wasn't receptive until you reached the bus station, which was across the railroad tracks from where you *say* you parked your vehicle."

"That's news to me," Rossi said.

"Are you saying you didn't know that, Peter?"

"That's what I'm saying. Why would I think the wire wasn't working? And for the second time my name is Pete."

The DA smiled at his own bullshit. "So you left the money in the car?"

Rossi answered hard. "Damn right. Bean told me if I tried anything he would kill my mother."

"Your mother?" Anderson took his eyes from Rossi, and then quickly began to rumble through his notes.

"That's right. My mother."

"Mr. Rossi, where does your mother live?"

"Belgium."

The DA thought his answer was hysterical and his punk laugh was annoying. He looked up from his papers and said, "And you feared for her life? All the way in Belgium?"

"So what of it? Crazy is crazy. I don't bet against crazy."

"Stop the games, Rossi. You were working undercover for narcotics and you stole city money and this is now a federal case. Have you ever done time, Peter?"

Rossi chuckled at Anderson's nerve. Anderson's attempt to get him upset was a no-go. I had heard that's how the prosecutors worked down-town—mainly on the brothers though. They liked to front on the accused and treat them with the least amount of respect possible to try and piss someone off to show how violent a person was. I was amazed Rossi was able to hold his temper. I don't think I could have handled Anderson that way. The white boy was smooth.

Rossi looked away from Anderson and turned his attention to Anderson's sexy assistant right after she stood up. I watched his eyes travel her body as she strutted over to the DA and patted him on the shoulder. Her body was delicious. Made me think of my girl Tammy and how long it had been since I'd had some. Tammy had been on my case for that very reason. She wanted to get laid. It had been weeks, but I had been busy getting my shop off the ground; twenty-hour workdays had been my norm.

Looking over the assistant DA, I couldn't get over how fine she was. The assistant had a round, delicate plump ass, perky stand-at-attention nipples and a dimple on the right side of her bronze baby-doll face. She whispered in Anderson's ear for a few minutes about the case and in between time, Anderson shot Rossi a few dirty looks. Finally, Anderson sat down. He looked as though he needed a stiff drink, perhaps even a double. That's when Allen took over.

"How are you today, Pete?" Assistant DA Allen wanted to know. Her voice was silky; I thought she was even flirting.

"Now you—you can call me Peter," Rossi told her. "But since you asked, I'm cool." Rossi gestured toward Anderson. "You need to check your boy though 'cause I didn't take any money and I think you believe that."

Allen smiled at Rossi. For my taste she was dressed much too sexy to be up in court. I wondered if her man had a problem with her wearing garments that let her nipples seep through her shirt. She looked like she was in her after-nine gear—like she was about to go to the club afterwards or go hang out with all those young executive types roaming Atlanta during *First Fridays* or something. But I had to give Allen her props. Her first name was Miea and I could truthfully admit Halle Berry didn't have one inch of beauty on her. Allen said, "First of all, out of all the people in the world, how were *you* chosen to do this sting operation?"

Rossi jumped right on her. "Chosen? I wasn't chosen. I was *made* to do it. Captain Stallings knew I had a court date coming up for possession of marijuana." Rossi looked at the jury to clarify his statement. "Look, the court date was for marijuana that *Stallings*, an officer for the City of Atlanta, had his officers plant on me one night after I *allegedly* blew a stop sign coming from the Waffle House after a night out on the town." Rossi looked directly at Anderson. "For the record, I want to mention the complaint against the officers I've filed with internal affairs to the grand jury as well. Captain Stallings and his men are who you should be investigating, not me because they planted the weed on me."

Allen interrupted; her voice was now three octaves higher. "Anyway," Allen said. She didn't want the jury to hear anything about police corruption, especially since all the television stations had been blasting the video of that young black cat getting his head smashed into the hood of a car out in California.

Rossi said, "What do you mean *anyway*? That's what happened. Captain Stallings comes to my house one night and tells me that if I participate in the sting, my drug case goes away. So I did it."

Allen sidestepped his corruption allegations. "So, you were born and raised in Hapeville, Georgia, right? Five minutes from city limits... right?" Rossi was too busy trying to look in between Allen's legs as the goddess sat directly across from him. His head was cocked to the side as though he was almost in and he just nodded his answer to her. I was sure that she even opened her legs for him once or twice trying to throw him off guard. "You need to answer (yes) or (no) Mr. Rossi," she told him.

"Ah, yeah. What's the question again?"

Allen made sure Rossi heard her the next time. "You-were-born-and-raised-in-Hapeville, right?"

"That's right."

"And that's where the drug deal was going down, right?"

"That's right."

"Tell us about living there."

"Nothing to tell. It's small. Not much to do and the Ford automobile plant takes up most of the city." Rossi settled in his seat. He was enjoying his view of Allen to the max.

She said, "So a small-town boy like yourself was able to gain the trust of two notorious drug dealers?"

Rossi chuckled. "I guess that's why your guys came to me in the first place, right?"

The alluring looks that the assistant shot at Rossi made me think she wanted to do ol' boy. "So how'd you do it? How'd you get them to trust you?"

"Mainly the pocket money Captain Stallings let me hold. It was thousands of dollars. As much money as I was blow'n, I think I could've taken you out." Rossi sat on the edge of his chair, smoothed out his tie, then pointed toward the jury. "Just to let you guys know, I accounted for every dollar that I spent to Captain Stallings who was the spearhead of this so-called drug bust every week." He smiled over at Anderson. "Just to let you know," he reiterated.

"*Anyway*...Rossi," Allen said. "How'd you gain their trust?"

"They owned strip clubs. Bean's place was near Midtown and Memphis down off Interstate 75. I went to both places on a daily basis, flashed a couple of ends and the word got back to them that a white boy was out on the floor spending mad dough." Rossi slapped his hands clean. "That simple," he boasted. I knew exactly the spot Rossi was telling the jury about. The name of it was Silk's. There were a few young cats that always came around while I fixed cars always talking about how good of a time it was. Tits everywhere and for a few extra ends—release and relief in a back room that was full of freaks.

Rossi ended up telling Allen that it took him two months to set up the drug deal and he didn't know exactly how much money he spent getting it done. Allen knew though. She said it was eighty thousand dollars. Rossi smiled in remembrance.

She asked him, "A person could get used to that type of money?"

"What do you think I'm going to say? You think I didn't enjoy spending that money? Well, I did. I enjoyed every dollar," he told her.

Allen verified that it was three hundred thousand dollars Rossi told the drug-dealing Bean that he wanted to spend on cocaine, and it was the amount of money put in his hands by the narcotics department then lost in the sting operation.

"That's exactly what Captain Stallings told me to tell him," Rossi explained. "Three hundred bills was our agreement."

Then Allen made sure that Memphis was the supplier and was supposed to receive the bundle of cash in exchange for narcotics. Rossi verified her claim. "Before the deal went down, you took the money, didn't you?" Allen slipped in.

"Look, you're fine. But you ain't that fine," Rossi answered. "I didn't take a damn thing. But I will take you to dinner tonight and that's for sure."

2

After Rossi's dinner date request to the assistant DA hot mama, District Attorney Anderson stood up with his scrawny ass and demanded everyone on the grand jury return the following Monday. He told us there was more testimony to come and afterwards we would vote on whether or not there was enough evidence to take Rossi to trial. Everything was clear to me. The DA's office wasn't satisfied that they couldn't break their boy and thought bringing everyone back was going to piss us all off, and then we would vote in their favor so they could send him to trial, then up the creek to be a bitch in prison. At that point, their plan worked for me because I was beyond pissed. I was being kept a prisoner of the system and I wasn't even on trial.

I gathered my things and darted out of the room before anyone else could leave. I wanted to get back to living my life. I had way too many things to do. Important things like make my rent and fixing the cars that were left in my bay. When I stepped out of the elevator that led to the parking garage I stopped at the sound of my name. I turned to look. It was Lauren. She was the only other black dot on the grand jury. I knew she was a bit younger than I was but I didn't know by how many years. She had sat next to me on the grand jury for the entire week. I didn't know why she was calling. My first thought was maybe I'd left something behind.

Lauren seemed to be one of those around-the-way girls—petite, peanut butter-colored with plenty of attitude if she was pushed to show it, but in my estimation she could stand to gain a few pounds. She wore her hair in braids and had a collection of jeans that looked as though they were spray-painted on her little plump ass. Lauren's eyes were wide and wondrous, most of the time—but she was quiet and seemed as though something pressing was always on her mind even during the brief conversations we would have during a break or between cases. Her cheekbones made Lauren stand out and added some uniqueness to her being. They were high and defined to the bone. Lauren never said much but I had a feeling she thought she looked good in her jeans. By the second day of jury duty, I was used to hearing her whisper her favorite saying about how disgusting or crazy some of the people were. *"These people have no shame,"* she would say. When she caught up with me, I asked her what she wanted.

For some reason Lauren looked around before she spoke back to me. When she finally did, her voice was barely over a whisper. "West, do you really mean what you wrote in your notepad back in there?"

She caught me off guard with her question. "Say what?"

"That Rossi's lying... it's what you scribbled in your notebook. I saw it."

"Oh my damn. You were all in my *B.I.* (business), weren't you? You need to be work'n for the police department."

"Well, you wrote it big enough for me to see."

"It wasn't meant for your eyes. It came from boredom."

Lauren prodded, "So you think he's guilty?"

I put my head down and started to walk away from Lauren. She knew damn well that we couldn't talk about the case. Talking about cases meant jail time. I wasn't going to jail and miss even more days from my shop. I wasn't the one to get caught up.

"West? Hold up a second," she called out again.

I looked back and she ran to catch up with me. I looked around the parking lot for two things: my car and to make sure that no one was watching me having a conversation with Lauren. On the very first day of jury duty, the clerk made it clear that we were being watched at all times and any questionable activity or conversations between jurors would be investigated.

"I think he's lying, too," she said.

"Oh, hell no," I told her. "You ain't getting me tossed in jail standing out here talk'n about this shit." Lauren's face dropped and I heard her exhale when I turned and walked away. I became confused when I didn't see my car where I parked it, so I stopped to take a look around.

"You gonna tell me if you do or not?"

I looked behind me and Lauren was standing actually waiting for me to answer her. But I refused. I wanted to get in my car, plop my Frankie Beverly CD in my player, and just drive away. I was sure I was standing exactly in the spot where I had parked my car because I had been parking there the entire week.

Lauren continued to harass me. "So you're not gonna answer me then—hunh?"

"Look, I don't care about that fool. If you think he's guilty, vote on it when we get back Monday."

I still hadn't found my car.

There was a car that passed us as we stood in the parking lot and Lauren moved closer to me and lowered her voice again, "West, I think we should find the missing money."

That's when I really took a good hard look at Lauren. Her words took me away from finding my car and having to return on Monday. "Do what?"

"You heard me. Let's find out where the money is. All week long, I've been inside there listening to you mumbling to yourself and watching you scribble down how much money you're losing by having to serve on jury duty. Now here's our chance to do something about it."

"What's this *we* and *our* shit? Ain't no *we* or *our*; my woman's at home." I scanned over the lot again. "Where is my... car?"

"C'mon, my car is right down here." Lauren pointed. "I'll drive you around and help you look for it," she offered. "I do this all the time, too...forget where I parked."

"I didn't forget. I parked my car right around here," I told her.

She adjusted her bag on her shoulder and said, "Well, where is it then?"

"I don't know, damn it."

Lauren started to walk away and even in my situation, I decided to take the time to travel Lauren's sculptured backside and the tight jeans that were plastered on her booty. The gap between her legs as she walked away triggered a thought in my head that whoever was bang'n her probably didn't have any trouble going all the way up inside her and hitting home plate. Lauren didn't even turn around while she spoke. "It's hot as hell out here, West. Coming or what?"

I looked around a few more times, and then I followed Lauren to her car. Maybe I did forget. Since I received the letter to appear for jury duty, things had been slipping my mind including my gas and phone bills— even my car payment. I decided to ride with her. Lauren drove me around the entire parking complex. About ten flights and hundreds of cars later and my vehicle was nowhere to be found. Lauren stopped her car where I told her I parked my car in the first place—then I got out. "Son of a bitch!" I realized my 1979 Caddy Coupe Deville had been stolen.

3

So, now my car was stolen. Not a damn place to be found. I wasn't used to being violated like that. Even though I lived in the hood people knew what was mine and kept their hands off my shit outta respect. All the years when I didn't have my shop and repaired cars right on the street by the curb for extra cash, I could leave all my tools out overnight and every last one would be there in the morning in the exact order I had left them. I had lived on my block for a while and with time came my respect in the streets. But as soon as I venture out to the city when I didn't even want to in the first place, I get my car stolen. I was heated and three clicks past pissed. My car meant the world to me and it was gone. Then to sprinkle the extra bull on my situation I now had to keep my shop closed one more day because the ball-busting match between Rossi and the DA wasn't over—and it made for an extra tight situation that I was in.

I couldn't help to blame the judge for my predicament. When I told him during the jury selection that my shop was my livelihood and I was my only employee to work it, he pissed me off with his *"why you telling me"* looks. The judge told me, "'I was outta luck because I was serving no matter what else I had to do." Fucker didn't care that my place of business wasn't some fly-by-night-waste of time venture. It did more than offer a service to the peeps in the community. It showed them they could open up their own establishments, too—but he couldn't see that.

Before I even opened my shop, sometimes I would chuckle at the thought of my black ass trying to set an example for some damn body to follow but I was— and I felt good about it. I was trying to show black folks on my block that they could have their own establishments also. I had seen way too many other minorities come in our community and set up shop and make plenty of money just the same.

My shop had been carefully planned out. I saved every penny I could to buy my equipment and open it up. I knew I still was going to have a hard time paying the rent, but it wouldn't have been a thought if it weren't for jury duty. If I had to, I could finagle my landlord Mr. Merrick for the rent but I didn't like doing that. At least not starting off. I didn't want to be one of those "check's in the mail" Negroes. I wanted to run my business legit and pay the man his rent like I told him I would on time.

"You sure do get quiet when you're mad, don't you?" We were about ten minutes into our ride. I didn't answer Lauren. I wanted to finish my cigarette and get home and down the bottle of whiskey in my cabinet. "My father used to do the same thing when he was upset. But guess what?" I wasn't interested but I asked her what the hell was she talking about anyway. "That shit only builds stress. Go 'head and scream if you want to; this car has wonderful acoustics."

Lauren wasn't going to leave me alone so I opened up. "Don't you know I just put new tires on my car? The engine was running like a smooth glass of cognac and I only had five more payments. I can't believe you sit'n up in here talking about screaming; I feel like whoop'n some ass—I really do." I went back to my smoke but I didn't like the way Lauren looked at me out the corner of her eye while she drove. "What?"

"You have *five* more payments on a nineteen-seventy-nine car?" Lauren was so small that she continuously moved her little body around in the driver's seat to get comfortable.

"That's right and no insurance," I let her know. "I'm fucked."

Lauren chuckled. "Don't stress, who has insurance these days?"

I sat up a bit from my slouched position to keep an eye on Lauren as she drove. "Just get me home safe. Shit, the way my day is going the next thing on the agenda for me is one of those head-on collisions then a life flight in a helicopter that runs outta fuck'n gas." I looked around for Lauren's seat belt so I could strap it on but she told me it was broken.

"What kinda car you say you have again?"

"You mean *had*," I reminded. "Seventy-nine Coupe Deville Caddy."

Lauren snickered. "Did it have a diamond in the back?"

"Oh, so this is like a joke to you—hunh?"

"Well, did it?"

"It's the only way to ride."

"That used to be my shit, used to sing that song all the time with one of my mother's boyfriends—that is until he tried to put his hands on me. *Diamond in the back…sunroof top*."

"You need to just let up. I gotta get my vehicle back."

"I can't believe you were still making payments."

"Bought it two years ago. Paid a little too much for it. But it's one of a kind. Why do you think it was stolen?"

Lauren was full of sarcasm. "I bet it is."

"You bet it is what?"

"One of a kind."

I looked around in Lauren's car. She had lots of nerve. She was pushing a rusted-out, early nineteen-eighty, caramel-colored Nova that needed an alignment like a mothafucka because I felt it pulling when she got up to around forty miles per hour. The rips in the seats looked as though a crackhead had gone to work on them looking for a next hit. Her hooptie had already seen its better days, probably two years after it was bought. "It's not like you're roll'n in one of them Navigators or some shit," I told her.

"I know; it's a hell of a place to have to live, isn't it? But I tell you one thing, this tub got me and my sister here safe and sound."

I took an extra long drag off my smoke. "Hey, I didn't know."

"How could you? I've been holed up here for the past two weeks. I got fired from JDS after they found out I didn't graduate from Georgia Tech. And just think, I was on my way to a promotion."

"I guess we both running a string of bad luck then. So where you from?"

"Charlotte by way of Cali. You?"

"From the deep woods of Georgia, where the poorest of poor live. Gonna be something though when my boys see me staggering back after all these years looking for some room in one of those shacks if I don't start making money at my shop. So why'd you move to Atlanta?"

"Get away from my mother. Start something new with my sister. You know...work, make something out of my life and make my money. All I want is a nice place to stay, some money, another job and a man. And just to think, I auditioned and won a part in a movie for a pretty nice piece of change and didn't take it when I was out in Cali for this."

My curious one-eye look didn't go unnoticed.

"You don't have to believe me. I did."

"You won a part in a movie?"

"Sure did."

"So why didn't you take it?"

"The producers wanted to fuck me."

"Say what?"

"Yup—husband and wife."

"How much was the part worth?"

"Thirty thousand."

The way she answered I couldn't help but to believe her. "And you didn't do it?"

"Unh...unh—my stuff is priceless."

I let the coochie price slide. I usually wouldn't let the opportunity get away to talk to a woman about how good she thought her loving was, but I wasn't feeling the conversation. "So where's your sister?"

"Don't wanna talk about her," Lauren said.

"Your choice, but I tell you this. You're in the right place if your head is screwed on right. With the right hustle you can do just about anything you want in this city."

"I think I do."

I flicked my smoke out the window. "I meant legally, 'cause I know you're about to say something else about that punk on grand jury and the money."

"Since you brought it up, I'm going to find Rossi before the weekend is over and see if he'll break me off," she told me. "Ain't no way I'm gonna let that easy money get away."

"I just want to know, what would make you come up with such a crazy idea anyway? You must be fuck'n desperate."

"No, just in a desperate situation. We all are. Plus, I've always been a fan of *what if*."

"What if what?"

"Exactly." Lauren read my face before she made a right-hand turn. I wasn't sure what the hell she was talking about. "I mean in life, baby. I like to wonder what would be if people would take risks in situations. Shit, most of the movies out nowadays, I've envisioned in my head years ago."

"Well, here's a thought. Write a damn movie then."

"Unh, unh, I don't have the patience," Lauren said. Then she started to babble about her plan that she claimed popped into her mind when she noticed I wrote down that Rossi was lying.

As we chatted, Lauren's roguishness seeped out of her. I didn't think she was a bad person but she was really intense and almost to a point of crisis—to make her conditions better. I guess to her anything would be worth trying—to have to not live in her car. But I was being careful talking to Lauren. In the back of my mind I was thinking this whole ride and conversation with Lauren could have been a set-up. Maybe the government would intentionally put my black ass in limbo because they couldn't make the case against Rossi and picked me as their stoolie because one of their cameras in the jury room noticed how impatient I seemed to be to get the hell out of there. I studied Lauren. I wasn't taking the chance. Whatever her angle, I wasn't buying. While we rode, Lauren was adamant that Rossi had the money or knew exactly where it was. Then she started shooting off about some plan of convincing the jury to vote not guilty for a cut of Rossi's money. I did tell her one thing though. I told Lauren that she had a better chance of getting a man, a job and a new place to stay, all in one day before her plan would ever work. Then I told her to forget about it and just get me home so I could have at my whiskey. I thanked Lauren for the ride and she was on her way.

4

I approached the door to my place cautiously hoping my girl Tammy had forgotten about the promise I made to her to run to the grocery store. She had told me earlier that day during one of my breaks that she was hungry and tired of looking into an empty fridge and snacking on my Sunshine cheese crackers. When I told her not to go in the refrigerator then she wouldn't know there wasn't anything to eat, she told me to kiss her ass, and get ready to spend some cash because she wanted some food up in our place or she was leaving until I went out and bought some.

I was one foot inside the door.

She said, "You ready to go?"

"Would you stop being so damn ghetto, Tammy? Can a brutha get a drink? Jack'n me at the door. You got your bag on your arm and jacket all buttoned up. What if I would have come home sick or something?"

"Ghetto? Nigga, please. Yeah, that's where I'm from and I claim mine. Plus you look fine to me so stop with the so tired mess. You ain't been doing nothing today but sit'n on your black ass."

"I need a drink."

"When we get back, West," she demanded.

"From where?"

"West, please don't start with me. There's nothing in this house to eat and you know I don't eat out, so let's go."

"You ain't got to worry about eatin' out 'cause I ain't got no money anyway," I told her.

"I'm just say'n, West."

I walked around Tammy and I went to my bottle of whiskey. I didn't even bother looking for a glass to pour it in.

"I just want to go get some food to put in this place, that's all."

After I took a huge swig and put the bottle on the countertop I told her, "Can't do it."

"What?"

"Can't. Somebody stole my fuck'n car."

"What the hell you mean somebody-stole-the-car?" Tammy went to the door, opened it and looked down by my shop where I always parked my baby.

"Somebody took my vehicle and I ain't got no wheels," I let her shocked face know.

"How'd you get here then?"

"Gotta ride."

I moved all the shit Tammy had on my couch. She spent her time (her so-called job) folding newspapers for a few dollars for some punk who was slinging papers to some of the major grocery store chains around the city. The nigga was fronting because I had a sense that he was into some illegal shit. I made it clear to Tammy that the mothafucker could throw some work her way, but he'd better not bring any illegal commotion over my house or that was his ass.

His name was Todd. A young slick, light-skinned buster who didn't fake me out one bit. I don't even know how Tammy met him. She was thirty-eight and he looked about thirty-five. I knew he wasn't really paying Tammy four to five hundred a month to fold any freaking newspapers. I had a gut feeling they were messing around behind my back, too. It wasn't like I didn't care because one thing I definitely didn't share was the pussy I was hitting, but I had been too busy getting my shop together to even think about what they were doing or to investigate. All I knew was they just better not let me catch them if they were.

"So what you gonna do now?"

"'Bout what?"

Tammy sat next to me and said, "About the car, nigga?"

"Don't know. But I gotta figure out something though."

"At least you can get back to work now. Mrs. Bullock has been over here twice talking about she needs her car back."

"Maybe I can finish her car this weekend but I have to go back on Monday."

"Damn, West, for what?"

"To finish up, Tammy. We've been called back. I told you I shouldn't have called them assholes when they sent me that notice for jury duty."

"I keep telling you, my girl didn't call after they summoned her and she found her ass up in jail."

"How long she get?"

"Two days."

"I should have gone to jail." And that's exactly the way I felt about my situation.

➤ ➤ ➤

After I finished off my whiskey I made my way up underneath Mrs. Shirley Bullock's car. She was one customer that I definitely didn't want to lose because of bad service. She drove a cherry-red, nineteen-seventy-eight Chevy Impala that her late husband kept in prime condition before his death after a bout with cancer. I had known her close to three years. When I first met Mrs. Bullock she was ten seconds away from getting taken advantage of at an auto repair shop that also sold parts. When I overheard the mechanic quote her a price for service, I followed her out and before she drove away I let her know I could do the work on her car for a hell of a lot cheaper than she was quoted: She took me up on my word.

It just so happened that Mrs. Bullock was a very important woman in Atlanta. Her late husband was a major player in city politics and the Bullocks knew everybody who was anybody in town. Mrs. Bullock's car needed a simple alignment and oil change but to Mrs. Bullock I was doing major surgery and it probably seemed like it. I had her car for more than a week because of jury duty. I didn't blame her though. She missed her car. I knew how she felt because I missed mine, too, and it only had been stolen a few hours. I managed to calibrate one tire on the Chevy before my shop phone rang.

"West?"

"Speak'n. Who's this?" I slurred. It had been a long day and my drinks were catching up with me. For a moment I thought it was Denise who stayed down the block from me. She and I had been making eyes and I knew if I got the chance I was going to go for it. The last time I saw her at the corner package store, her looks were telling me she was ready to give me some of her brown sugar and I slid my number into the bag that was hugging up close to her tits.

"Lauren," the voice said on the other end.

"Lauren?"

"I got your shop number from info. Listen, you remember what I told you about my plan?"

"No."

"About finding Rossi."

"What about it?"

"I know where he is right now," she said.

"How do you know where he is?"

"Nigga, I know. That's all you need to know."

"So what?"

"So, I've been thinking about the plan where we can get at least half the money."

"*We?* Whatever, Lauren, I'm busy right now."

"How 'bout I come pick you up and I tell you all about it."

"Not interested."

"Look, I know you're not as weak as you're acting, West. Let me tell you something. That shit you're living in ain't no better than the car I sleep in."

"Forget about where I live. Wait a minute—who are you calling weak? Lauren, I'm a grown-ass man."

"You're a weak man, and old and ain't ever gonna have shit unless you take it."

I looked into the phone not believing her boldness. "Who you calling *old*?" I heard her laughing on the other end. "You."

"Me?"

"You heard me, old man."

"How old do you think I am?"

"Shit, I don't know. Forty-nine goin' on fifty maybe? I can't really tell because of that one-inch-thick mustache on your lip and the derby hat you're rocking."

"You talking about me like you know me or something."

"Plus, you're really dark-skinned and ya'll hold up pretty good."

Lauren had plenty of nerve. "See, your young ass don't know shit, Lauren. I'm forty-two."

"Wow, you look much older." We were quiet for a few seconds. Lauren said, "Now listen, he's at a titty bar downtown."

My buzz from the whiskey put an image in my head: young, vibrant, freaky women saying nothing but showing every nook and cranny. The whiskey told me it was just what I needed to help me drown my sorrows of losing my car and another day of jury duty—even though I didn't have a dime for the rump shakers. "He's in a strip joint, you say?"

"Yep. He just went inside to get his eyes full."

"Fuck it. Pick me up in twenty minutes."

5

Luckily Tammy went down the street to see a girlfriend five minutes before Lauren pulled up to my place, close to ten o'clock that night. That way I didn't have to hear a bunch of questions about where I was going with a woman that she didn't know. Before she left I gave Tammy a few dollars and told her to get whatever she could with it at the store, then I showered and put on a simple button-down shirt and pants.

I have to admit Lauren cleaned up well, and it was sort of a surprise to see her looking so good. She had on a pair of super-tight black jeans and a tight black shirt that exposed her nipples on her small chest. She didn't seem to feel as odd as it really was looking at her did-up so fly. She was very comfortable with her outfit she was rocking.

"So what made you change your mind?" Lauren wanted to know as soon as I shut the car door. "Was it because I called you *old*?"

"Naa…"

She smiled. "Yes, it was, old man."

"It wasn't. Can you stop with the *old man* shit? How old are you anyway?"

"In my thirties."

"Thirty what?"

"Thirty-two going on twenty-two and looking what would you say?" She looked over her body with a quick glance. "Twenty-eight, maybe?" Lauren pulled up from her seat to look at me. "What's wrong? It looks like I just took all the air out of you."

"I'm cool. Just haven't been out in a while," I told her, but actually our age difference was a bit of a shock.

"So, you only goin' with me for a free ride to go see some jiggling breasts since your car got stolen or to talk to Rossi?" I didn't answer. I just slid down into the front seat to enjoy the ride. "Tell me something? How old are you really, West?"

She was beginning to annoy me with the age questions. "Why?"

"'Cause I'm tryin' to figure out why you're frontin' like you're squeaky clean. I can tell you've done dirt before."

"I've done plenty. But I like my freedom. And what's the use do'n dirt when you gotta walk around wonder'n if you gonna get caught?"

And plenty of dirt I had done. The reason I moved from Preston, Georgia going on close to eleven years in the first place—was because I beat the shit out of this sucker after he caught me cheating in a game of craps. There was no way I could stay in Preston, after what I did. I was either going to jail for the beat-down or six feet under 'cause I had heard through family—his boys still hadn't forgotten about my dirty deed.

Lauren started in with her sarcasm again. "Oh, so you have morals."

"Look, I'm forty-two, okay? Maybe you'll understand why I like my freedom so much when you live a little—and why'n the hell we talk'n 'bout me so much? I don't know you like that, Lauren. All I know about you—is that you sit next to me on jury duty. How do I know you ain't one of those women that gets niggas thrown in jail doing twenty-year bids for some change in your pocket? Coming up with all these crazy ideas and shit."

"'Cause I ain't."

"But I don't know that. I don't trust like that; matter of fact, stop this fuck'n car."

"What?" Lauren kept her eyes on the road and the car moving.

I turned to her and took my smoke out of my mouth, then gritted my teeth. "I said, stop this car." When she stopped, I started going through her car like I had lost a winning lotto ticket. I lifted up the clothes in her back seat—looking for a hidden camera or wire and through her glove box for any kind of electronic device.

"Nigga, what're you doin'?" Lauren said. "In here fuckin' up my car.

What're you looking for?" I stopped and looked Lauren over. "What?…
What, nigga?" she repeated.

"Pull up your shirt."

"Nigga, what?"

"Pull your shirt up. I wanna see if you're wired. Out here talking about
doing felonies and shit. Pull the mothafucka up or I'm walk'n."

Lauren smiled, and then shook her head. "Okay, nigga, if you want me
to pull up my shirt so you can get a thrill, here. Have at it. See, no wire
here." Lauren ran her hand over both her small black tits. "Or here."

"Good."

"Have you seen enough 'cause I could stay like this all night—then you
don't even have to go to the titty bar."

Lauren was being sarcastic. I turned my head away. But she didn't
budge until I looked at her again. "Okay, okay, put your shirt down. I
already told you—I don't trust too well."

Lauren became quiet and looked at me a few times as she drove. I was
two small drags from the end of my smoke. She said, "Look, I've done
some shady things in my life, okay. Things that I ain't proud of, but I'm
no stool pigeon and I don't put black men in jail. I just see an opportunity,
that's all."

"An opportunity, hunh?"

"That's right. We help him and he helps us."

"And what the hell can we do for him?"

"Look, we can get his lying ass off and save his pretty behind from having
to bend over every night in prison, that's what."

"How?"

"Haven't you been listening to me?"

"Not really."

"Get the jury to vote 'no bill' so he walks. That's how."

"Now I'm sure you're crazy."

"Please. I'm a hell of an actress and can get people to do anything I
want. You should at least know that 'cause I have your ass 'bout to go up
in here with me."

"Look, I'm go'n to get the edge off. It's been a rough day."

"Whatever, West. What I have planned is gonna take two to get things done."

"To do what?"

"Persuade the jury to let his ass walk, that's all. But first things first; we've gotta let Rossi know we'll do it for a slice of that money he got stashed."

"How much you talking 'bout?"

"I'm thinking fifty percent of what he's got. Then we split it fifty-fifty and go our separate ways."

"You must be out your mind."

"Nigga, I'm in the right frame of mind. It would be a nice payday." She looked over at me. "Everybody needs a bailout, West. The airlines got 'em after nine-one-one. People get bailouts all the time. Why can't we get one to bail us out of our financial situations?"

6

Oh, my damn. The music in the club couldn't have been any louder. *Bump, Bump, Bump, Bump* hit me in the face at the door and was blaring in every direction throughout the club. That's when I thought twice about what the fuck I was doing before I gave the big ugly mug at the door my five dollars to get in and let him search me with his metal detector all around my nuts. But with Lauren's prodding and a sly peek through the door of the babes sliding up and down the brass pole on center stage as they opened their legs and snatched up dollars with the greatest of ease, I decided I could make due with the ear-aching sounds blasting through the speakers and Lauren's half-baked plan to present to Rossi. Before we decided to take a table, we stood for a while in a busy aisle as Lauren scanned the joint for Rossi. Then a slender white girl in a g-string and puffy melons under a powder-blue negligee greeted us with a strip-joint smile.

"My name is Passion," she said. "What can I get you two to drink?"

Passion was about an inch or two shorter than me and stood about five feet nine. Her body was all butter. She was put together nicely and the see-through negligee she sported showed just enough of everything she had to offer. Lauren ordered a whiskey sour. I wanted mine straight with one ice cube. Passion led us to a table and told us she'd be back in a flash as she shot us a seductive look, then strutted away.

Lauren was hyped because I could hear her clearly over the music. "This is fun. Might as well have some fun while we're here."

I guess Lauren started to look for Rossi again, but my eyes were focused on the girls. All of them were fine. The club was definitely hot. Men were tossing bills to the dancers and the girls were giving them a look at their bodies from every angle. I never totally understood what made some women play themselves by shaking their bare asses for any nigga who would throw a dollar bill in their direction. But at that moment, I wasn't mad at them not one freaking bit because I definitely understood why the niggas were inside spending cash because the sight of the ladies made instant boners.

"Okay, guys, I'm back!" Passion announced before she sat down our drinks. She looked at me just before I took a sip of my drink. "Would you like a dance?"

My answer was a no-brainer; I had no cash.

I don't even think my tongue had a chance to taste my drink before Lauren spewed out, "I would!"

Passion's eyes extended. "Really?"

"Sure would. Drop it like it's hot!" Lauren punched.

"Oh, it's hot," Passion promised. "Just wait, you'll see."

Passion smiled at Lauren, and then put her tray on our table. Lauren looked at me and shrugged her shoulders with widened eyes. Passion stepped back from the table a few feet and looked at Lauren and twirled around for her slowly, giving her every angle of her stacked body as the bass continued to pound the club. When she faced Lauren again, she took her exposed left melon from her top and grabbed it with her right hand and began to lick her lips. Lauren smiled and took a sip of her drink. Passion turned around, looked back at Lauren then bent down and touched her ankles, then whipped and jiggled her plump ass in front of Lauren. I looked around and all of a sudden our table was the center of attention in our section. When Passion strutted over to Lauren's chair and mounted Lauren with her legs spread wide, and began to gently grind on Lauren's middle section, onlookers downed more drinks and yelled with pleasure.

"Oh, my goodness, work it, girl!" Lauren told Passion right before she stood again and lifted her negligee to show Lauren some of her bare ass.

When the music stopped, Passion kissed Lauren on the cheek. Lauren tried to give Passion a couple of bills, but Passion wouldn't take them.

"Please don't leave here without getting my number," Passion pleaded to Lauren. "You're hot." Then Passion sashayed her way to another table full of men waving plenty of cash who had been watching her work her magic with Lauren.

A few minutes passed.

Lauren looked over at me. "What are you lookin' at?"

"I didn't know you were off limits all a sudden."

"You can say it," she said. "Don't matter to me."

"Okay, I will. You're wild. Fuck'n out of control."

Lauren looked at me like I didn't have a clue, then sat up closer to me. "Tell me something, West. You ever moved into a new place and it wasn't exactly sparkling clean? Maybe you had to repaint the walls or scrub the kitchen floor or something? Maybe even get down on your hands and knees and clean somebody else's scum from a tub?"

I flicked my smoke in an ashtray. "Evidently you didn't take a good enough look at the shit I'm living in."

"Well, then…I'm sure you can understand what I was doing then?"

"No, I can't because I think you were getting yo freak on. But shit, I don't need to understand. I mean if that's your thing…fine. Do the damn 'thang."

"Smart'n up, West. I'm strictly, okay?"

"Strictly, hunh? I don't know, for a while…"

"Good, I'm glad it worked."

"What?"

"The dance with Passion. I was getting things ready for us to move in. That dance with Passion was just a decoy to move into Rossi's life because I know he's in here and believe me he saw what just happened. He's a freak; I can tell by his eyes."

"So you say'n you didn't enjoy that?"

Lauren smiled. "Did you?"

➤ ➤ ➤

We sipped on our drinks and I remembered from what Rossi told the grand jury, a thug called Memphis once owned the club we were in. From what I could see, even bigger money had taken it over. Passion came around a time or two to check on our drinks. She gave Lauren her telephone number and teased her once during an R. Kelly slow jam, then disappeared into the smoke of the club. She returned five minutes before we were about to call it a night because Rossi was nowhere in sight.

"Hey, baby, someone wants to see you and your friend in VIP," Passion told Lauren.

"Who?" Lauren asked.

"He didn't say. Said he knew you guys and wanted to know if you would have a drink with him."

Lauren looked over at me. "Sure. Lead us to him."

7

The VIP section was popping inside. Ass, tits, bodacious bodies standing on stilettos were everywhere, in every corner of the section waiting to serve those who had enough to pay what it cost for the goodies inside. I only had one complaint; there wasn't enough lighting so I could see all of the fine woman who were lounging about on the cream-colored leather chairs playing host in their thongs. There were clans of shapely females who were much too fine to touch the brass pole out in front of the club waiting for the next baller to stroll through the door of VIP. They even had large pillows sprawled across the room as players sat with girls in their laps, some even on their backs; no doubt being tongue serviced for a fee as they sipped champagne and stiff drinks. Passion finally stopped at a booth lined with curtains and pulled them back.

"If it isn't my grand jury," Rossi said. This muthafucka looked as though he didn't even have a case hanging over his head. He didn't seem worried one bit that he could be another step closer to prison in a matter of days. "C'mon in, you two."

Rossi was dressed to a tee: in a nicely tailored deep blue, pinstriped suit with open collar. There were three women sitting at his table. The chick sitting closest to him was white: almond eyes, blonde hair with a nice tan and she didn't have on a shirt. Her nipples were hard and long—saying hello to me. The other two freaks—one black who I could tell had eaten plenty of red beans and rice coming up because her body was hitting on all cylinders; and the other girl who was mixed but yet still fine as hell, with silky, blue black hair—sat very close together.

Rossi noticed Lauren's hesitance after his invite to sit. "It's okay," he said. "Everyone here are guests of mine. I even own the small bar tonight. Can I get you anything?"

After I made sure he knew our names, I told him whiskey and he talked Lauren into getting a steak and baked potato to munch on. After a few minutes of small talk, I was getting used to having the girls around, especially after the two I was sitting in-between began pressing their mountains toward my chest, while I sipped my drink. But much too soon, Rossi asked them to leave.

As they left our small gathering, Rossi lit a cigar and kind of smiled. "Don't mind me, I'm just fronting." He laughed. "I usually don't smoke these but they just enhance the atmosphere." Rossi lit up nicely and through the smoke said, "Ya'll here to see me or just to enjoy the view?" Lauren told him to take a guess. Rossi smiled. "Something told me somebody on the grand jury had some smarts."

He offered me a Cuban and I accepted. All of a sudden I had a feeling Lauren was looking to me to take charge of her plan like I was—the mastermind behind us really sitting down with Rossi because she wouldn't take her eyes off me. So I did. I asked Rossi what he meant by *smarts.*

"You know, some heart, some street knowledge. I just knew someone was sitting on the grand jury who really understood their opportunities with my case. It definitely was a vibe in that room."

I hadn't decided to partake in Lauren's scam before I sat down with Rossi. But really seeing the opportunity up close and personal made me think we could possibly pull off a serious coup if planned exactly right. Then I began to think—how in the world else would I ever get a chance of making so much money so quickly. I definitely didn't see a huge fleet of cars coming into my shop to be repaired in the future. Looking at Rossi and his calculated moves and statements to the girls who had just left the table, I was sure he had the money—he denied having to the grand jury; but he had yet to admit it. Then it happened.

"I'm not going to dance around with this," Rossi said. "I know why you came and you both know what I need. As long as we can come up with a fair deal, I don't think there will be a problem with making this thing happen."

> ➤ ➤ ➤

On the ride back home Lauren was hyped and she even tugged with me a bit saying, "Hey, West? I didn't see you focusing too much on the ass back there. What's the matter? You scared of a little ass?"

"I enjoyed myself—believe that. Ain't no need of really look'n if you can't touch."

"Oh, you like to do the do, hunh?"

"You better ask somebody," I told her. "All I have on my mind is what the hell we're getting ourselves into."

"Don't worry. I told you—that white boy was scandalous," Lauren boasted. "He wants to stay out of jail, keep that money and doesn't mind breaking us off in the process."

"But we only have two days to figure out how we're going to do this. It's back to jury duty on Monday."

"Well, all that money is motivation enough to get it done." Lauren pumped on the brakes a few times for no damn good reason.

"Take it easy...you're destroying my high."

She looked over at me. "You know he's lucky we're not asking for more. Freedom is a hell of a price. Maybe we should just go three ways straight down the middle? We all get equal parts instead of us getting crumbs."

"Fifty-fifty is cool, definitely more than we had. If we pull it off, we'll get seventy-five grand a piece. Believe me, I'm cool with that."

"Aww, he'll take it. He doesn't have a choice or we'll send his ass to prison and he'll wish he would've taken our offer," Lauren promised. "Damn, power feels good, don't it?"

"Look, you need to chill. Maybe I should go alone and meet with him tomorrow night if you gonna get all power-struck over this."

"Forget that? This was my idea, West. We do it together. I stay in the loop, nigga."

"I think I should do it. Alone."

"You must be out your mind. First you wanted no parts; now you want to run shit."

"Well, soothe your mind, Lauren, 'cause we splitting fifty-fifty with him. Then down the middle between me and you."

Lauren looked at me hard. "Whatever." Then she turned off I-75 two exits from my place.

"What are you doing? My exit is two up."

"I need to see something; won't take but a second."

"Like what—this late at night?"

Lauren didn't answer. I slid down into her seat and decided to enjoy my buzz. She looked over at me twice before the car began to slow down. We ended up on the West Side of town cruising slow and very careful. After five minutes I was damn near sleep but I heard her exhale, then slam the car into park. Her door was open and she was out the door and walking down the street before I could rise up and see what the hell was going on. It took me a minute to get my vision together but Lauren was on the street corner talking to some chick. The first thing that went through my mind was that she was out there dime'n me out to another undercover agent about all the shit that had gone down at the strip joint. There was no way I was going to be sitting up in jail the rest of the weekend waiting to get processed Monday morning over a conversation with Rossi. So I eased out the car without anyone noticing and got closer to them to hear exactly what they were talking about—because if Lauren was talking to the police, my drunk ass was going to run like a son of a bitch.

"Okay, c'mon, come back, Lauren..." the woman pleaded after Lauren took a step away from her.

"Lex, didn't I tell you to stay the fuck out these streets?" Lauren asked.

"I know, but what am I supposed to be doing? I don't have no money, no place to stay except in the back seat of your car. Fuck that; I gotta make ends meet."

Lauren said, "Well, why you have to do it out here in the streets? At least have some decency about yourself. Shit—get a room at a hotel and do the tricks there instead of in their cars. You're going to get killed out here." The woman Lauren was talking to had on a red dress and was holding a small handbag. Her stilettos couldn't have been comfortable because of the way she was leaning to her left side. I couldn't tell because of the lighting but she looked like she had a wig on.

"So who has your son?" Lauren wanted to know.

"He's over with Preach and them. I left him until the morning."

"Preach?"

"Yes, Preach. Don't start."

"Lex, you left my nephew with a crackhead?"

That's when I realized Lex must have been the sister Lauren didn't want to talk about.

Lex chuckled a bit. "Preach ain't no damn crackhead. I don't know why you think that."

"He smoke crack, don't he?"

"He used to smoke. But he don't no more."

"I'm getting so tired of your shit, Lex. Look, if you don't straighten up you might as well just stay out in these streets. And I am gonna call Defax on your child so the state can take care of him since you don't seem to give a fuck about him."

Lex moved closer to Lauren. "If you do anything to get my son taken away from me, Lauren, I-will-fuck-you-up."

Lauren pushed Lex. "Handle your business and I won't."

Lex lunged at Lauren.

I stepped out of the darkness.

"Yo, Lauren? You think you can get me home?"

They both stopped and turned to look at me.

"Oh, shit...what do we have here," Lex said.

"Look, a nigga need to get home all right. Maybe you can handle this another time?"

"Yeah, go 'head. Get the fuck outta here," Lex told Lauren.

Lauren seemed kind of surprised that I was around. "Yeah, sure, West. I will get you home." Then she turned to Lex. "You just make sure you call Preach and tell him I'm on my way to get Lil'Man, okay? And I will talk to your ass later."

"Whatever," Lex said.

Lauren started to walk to the car, but looked back. "I mean it, Lex, call him now!"

The only thing Lauren said to me on the way to my place was if she could hold a twenty to fill up her gas tank because she was going to have to leave the car running all night. I didn't hesitate to give her a twenty spot, especially if she was going to have a small child in the car with her all night.

After Lauren dropped me off, I swayed all the way up to my front door but I was under control. The whiskey had set in my system hard. It was cool outside. I flipped my collar up to my ears as I walked up the stairs to my apartment. It had been a long day. My car was gone. I wanted my bed. I thought maybe the next morning I would come to my senses and forget about Lauren and Rossi, then go back to my normal fucked-up life of trying to make an honest dollar. When I reached my door, I didn't get a chance to use my key to open it. It was snatched open right after I heard the last of Lauren's muffler scrape its way down the street as she zoomed off to wherever she was going for the night.

I knew I was in for some drama when my eyes focused in on Tammy standing in the doorway with her hand resting on her hip and she didn't waste any time with her loud ass voice. "Nigga, where have you been and who the hell was that?"

I looked her up and down. "Is that my robe? Why are you always wear'n my shit?"

She stepped closer to my face. "I know you're not drunk?"

"Nope, but damn near." I eased my way past her into my place.

"Well, you look like it. Who was that in that car, West?"

"A friend." I plopped down on the morning newspapers that needed to be picked up and delivered in a couple of hours.

"A friend? West, you don't have any friends, so don't give me that shit."

"But you sure do, don't you? You think I'm damn stupid, don't you, Tammy?" I looked around at the mess in my place. "Why would a nigga be giving you all this money to fold all these papers if you wasn't fuck'n him?" Then I threw what I could of the papers on the floor so I could rest my head.

"'Cause, nigga, I got it like that, that's why. So are you gonna tell me who the fuck that was in that car?" Tammy stood over me, hands on her hips, legs spread shoulder wide.

"Her name is Lauren. We got jury duty together."

"And?"

"And what?

"And what the fuck were you doin' with her, nigga?"

"We had to go check something out."

"Like what?"

"For the grand jury. Damn."

"Nigga, when the hell did the grand jury start workin' weekends?" Tammy sat next to me on the couch and sniffed my neck.

"Go on now, Tammy…" I moved away from her.

She sat still for close to ten seconds without a word. She was trying to read me and my drunk ass was trying to figure out what she was reading. "Fuck this," she said. Tammy went for my belt buckle to go down in my pants. "Did you fuck her, West?"

The liquor in my system made me laugh at her stupid ass question. "No—I ain't fuck her."

"Nigga, don't laugh at me. Are you sure? 'Cause you ain't been givin' me none lately," Tammy reminded me.

I tried to sit up but it wasn't happening. "And you know why, don't you?"

"Look, nigga, me and Todd are friends, okay? We ain't doin' nothing and don't try to flip the script on me. We're talkin' about your black ass."

I felt myself dozing off. "I said we didn't fuck, didn't I. Now I'm sleepy. I have something big to do tomorrow."

As I began to drift, I faintly heard Tammy yapping about Mrs. Bullock ringing my phone off the hook about her car along with my staying out all night and how Tammy was getting tired waiting on my dick and why the hell I wasn't giving her any. I faintly heard her say she was tired of playing with herself. Her mouth was moving much too fast for me because the liquor was now in control and wanted to put me to sleep and that's what it did. I'm sure Tammy didn't stop yelling until she was completely finished saying what she had to say.

8

It was past one in the afternoon when I finally dragged myself out of bed the next day. Sleeping the whole day could have been a possibility if it weren't for the crazy dream that made me sit straight up from my slumber. My dream had Tammy fucking her friend Todd in my kitchen and he was mocking and laughing at me—telling Tammy I was a sorry sucker while he was up in her pounding away—ass up over my kitchen table. After I got the whiskey aftermath from my mouth and took a nice hot shower, I walked into the kitchen and I be damned if that nigga Todd wasn't sitting at my kitchen table.

"Hey, baby," Tammy said. She was standing over the stove in a white apron that I bought her with bold red letters that said, "You Wanna Taste?" "You want something to eat? How 'bout some breakfast or lunch? We got it all up in here," she boasted.

No one had to tell me; my mouth was wide open with surprise as I scanned the kitchen. There were pancakes, eggs, grits, a jug of orange juice on my table and five more grocery bags full of shit sitting on my countertop. It looked like the Golden Corral up in my kitchen. Tammy had on her silk housecoat underneath her apron. I couldn't tell if she had on panties or a bra or what. I had a notion to walk over to her, rip her apron off, sling her housecoat open and put my finger inside her cat to see if she was wet or freshly fucked because the dream I had earlier was beginning to really annoy me.

That nigga Todd wouldn't even look at me as he sat at my table. I felt myself about to lose it because he wouldn't acknowledge me in my own damn house. He was pretending to count his freaking papers on the floor while he sat in a chair. By the second I was getting heated and thought about whooping on his scrawny two-bit, paper-selling cranium. All he had to do was say the wrong thing to me and it was on.

I looked hard at Tammy. "What's all this?"

"It's breakfast or how the white folks do it? Brunch, nigga." Tammy chuckled.

Todd looked over at her and smiled.

"No-no. Where-did-it-come-from? I didn't give you this much money for all of this."

"Todd brought it over for us."

I looked at Todd. He continued with his counting. "No, he brought it over for you—and can't you talk?"

Todd stopped his fake ass counting. "Look, man, I didn't mean any harm. Tammy said ya'll needed some groceries up in here so I hooked it up."

"Oh… is that right? So you just hooked it up?"

"That's right," Tammy said. "So don't get mad; be thankful, West." Tammy went back to pouring batter and flipping her pancakes.

I stood and thought *thankful* my ass. How did a nigga have the gall to bring groceries into another man's house for his woman? I was thinking that a beat-down was in order. I could tell Todd was uneasy about the way I stared at him. Every time I saw his punk ass he had a different look and that alone pissed me off. Sometimes he would have a mustache on his pretty-boy, light-skinned face. Other times he would sport the goatee or a light trimmed beard with no hair or the beard with a little on top of his head. Little did this punk know he was two seconds from getting served one of those freak'n link sausages he brought into my house shoved straight up his ass for real.

"Tammy, what happened to the money I gave you last night for food?"

"Me and Karla drank that shit up at the club on a bottle full of bub," she said.

I took a few steps toward Todd. "Look, nigga, I don't need your help, okay?" Tammy was about to open her wide mouth and say something to me. "No, Tammy, shut-the-fuck-up. This is my place. Respect my shit."

"Cool," Todd said. "It will never happen again." He picked up a few papers, told Tammy he would talk to her later and left.

I stood looking at Tammy standing over the stove for the longest without a word, then decided. "Make me five pancakes, sausage and some fuck'n cheese eggs." Then I poured myself a huge glass of orange juice.

Damn right I was eating.

> ➤ ➤ ➤

After I finished eating, I went back to bed to get some rest because I really didn't know how long I was going to be out with Lauren for our meeting with Rossi. I heard my front door open and I knew it was Todd again. He usually came over two, sometimes three times a day on Saturdays to bring the different sections of the huge Sunday paper. I went into my living room and Tammy was watching Todd bring the papers in. She looked back at me when Todd went out of the house again, hoping I wouldn't start any more shit with him. When Todd brought the last of the papers in he looked at my favorite chair and thought about sitting in it, but then flopped his ass on my couch and started to count his papers again. Tammy walked over to me.

"Whas' up, baby?"

"What you mean?"

She was easing up on me. Flirting no doubt. "I mean whas' up? You need anything? Anything to eat?"

Todd looked up at me. "Naa, I'm cool." I turned around and went back to my room. Before I could shut the door Tammy was standing at the door.

"West, baby, we gotta stop this fighting."

"Say what?"

"We can't be no item like this, baby. You—my man. I'm just trying to make money. That's all I'm trying to do. Times are hard."

"Yeah, they are, and that's why I am working on something really big right now, and I don't need any extra mess stressing me."

"What do you mean?"

"Nothing, forget about it."

"You mean with that chick that brought you home last night?"

I lay on the bed and clicked on the television. "I said, forget about it, Tammy."

Tammy sat next to me. "West, if we gonna be together, we have to trust each other. I know I was wrong for thinking you fucked her last night. I just wasn't used to you going out. You hardly ever go out—especially with another woman. You just ain't never did nothing like that before and it tripped me out."

She was right about that. I usually spent all my time in my garage. Fixing my cars, sipping on my yack and waiting to get my daily look at D who would from time to time switch past the shop to tease a brother.

"I just don't appreciate that nigga bringing food over here."

"I know. It was wrong. That was just foul, West, and it was all my fault because I urged him on."

"So ain't nothing go'n on between you two?"

"Nothing, nothing at all. We're just friends, West."

Tammy knew her words didn't comfort me and she stood up and took off her shirt. Her dark melons were standing at attention, and then she wiggled out of her tight jeans.

"Here, let me give you a little something," she said.

She was looking good, especially when she started to turn in circles showing me every bit of her thick chocolate body. Tammy took her melons and brought them up to her mouth and circled them with her tongue. When she did that, my stuff made its way through my pajama pants.

"What about your boy downstairs?"

"What about him? If I cared about him, you think I would do you—while he was here?"

I didn't even have time to think about her question. Tammy's mouth was already on me. She was alternating her mouth and her melons on my stick. She pushed me back on the bed and put herself on my boy who was fully awake, damn near to a point of aching.

"I wanna cum so bad—that I don't even need you inside me," she said. Tammy started to pump on me. A couple of minutes after I had a handful of her beautiful black behind in my grasp, she screeched, then jerked. She looked down at me with a smile. "See, I told ya. Did you feel that?"

"You popped that quick?"

Tammy said, "Sure did. Now it's your turn." Tammy moved her head down in between my legs and it wasn't long before I was satisfied, back in bed and asleep to get my rest for my busy night with Lauren and Rossi.

9

Lauren called around five in the afternoon from a Kinko's printing shop courtesy phone. She said she would be over around seven to pick me up. I told her it would be a good idea if she came in to say hello to Tammy this time.

When she arrived Tammy couldn't wait to pull that girlfriend routine on Lauren. No sooner than Lauren stepped in the door, Tammy was so full of compliments that she damn near embarrassed me, and I usually didn't care what came out of her mouth. She told Lauren that she really loved the makeup she was rocking, asked her if she was on some type of diet because she looked so thin and told her that she was thinking about getting her hair done in braids, too. Then to make matters worse, she tried to get into Lauren's personal life at the same time telling Lauren way too much about our relationship.

Lauren was soaking Tammy's shit up. Tammy almost got Lauren to open up to her in the spirit of sisterhood on what we had going on for the night. I stepped in just in time because Lauren fell for Tammy's plot and told Tammy what we were working on was something *really big*, which was way too much. After hearing that, I got dressed and pushed Lauren out of the door, then told Tammy I would see her later.

Tammy was looking down at us from the window in the apartment while Lauren tried to start her car. I took a few hits on my cigarette while Lauren tried to get her car to crank.

"Unh, unh, hell no. You givin' her too much gas," I told her.

Lauren was getting upset. I could tell she was thinking about what it meant if her car didn't start and we would blow the chance at the money. "You gonna tell me how to start my own shit?"

"I'm just telling you—you givin' her too much gas. Take your foot off the gas. She already got enough gas up in her." Lauren removed her foot, cranked it again and she started right up. "See, what I tell you?" I just happened to look at the gas gauge. "Are we riding on Eddie?"

"Gauge doesn't work—but I put in five before I got here."

I took one more glance at Tammy who was still in the window before Lauren pulled off. "Why'd you have to run your mouth back there?"

"What're you talking 'bout, West?"

"Look, this ain't nobody's business but ours, you hear? Nobody else needs to know about it."

"Stop buggin' out, damn. I didn't tell her about the deal with Rossi. All I said was we were working on something really big."

"You were about to, if I hadn't have stopped you."

"But I didn't. Did I? And Tammy's cool anyway."

"Yeah, she's cool all right. She runs her mouth too much. So leave her out of the loop, okay? I'm not try'n to get caught up messing with this fool if we can't make the shit happen. A nigga like me can't go to jail—you got that?"

"Well, I ain't trying to go either. So think positive."

I needed another smoke. My nerves were beginning to jump—so I took one out and fired up. "I don't even know why I'm doing this. I don't do shit like this?"

Lauren looked at me and said, "The same reason as me." Her voice raised a bit saying, "Nigga, don't get brand-new."

"Say what?"

"You're doing it 'cause you need the money. Point-blank, nothing more, nothing less."

"Fuck that, I got a business."

"But you ain't making no money, West. So get off it. By the way, what's the plan?"

"All of the sudden I got the plan?"

"I thought you did. You're the one who told him to meet us at the drive-in."

➤ ➤ ➤

Before we left the strip club Rossi agreed to meet us at the drive-in: in the back row of the parking lot of screen seven on Moreland Avenue. I didn't feel it was safe to meet him at the strip club again. I couldn't be sure if he was being watched or not. Once we arrived, Lauren couldn't wait to get some popcorn. I was licking my chops for the beer she brought along because I hadn't had a chance to see the movie *Training Day* and I thought I might as well enjoy myself. I was about fifteen minutes into the movie and about to open my beer when I realized Lauren hadn't made it back yet from the snack stand. We had a few minutes before we were to meet with Rossi so I went into the cinderblock-constructed, slick yellow-painted concession stand to see what the hell was taking her so long. I took one step inside and looked around. The only people inside were three workers behind the counter and a lady chasing her four little kids around while trying to handle four boxes of popcorn and drinks at the same time. I went back outside and walked around to the restrooms.

"Mothafucka, let me by!" I heard a voice say.

"Shut up, bitch," a voice answered.

I walked up close enough to see what was going on. I could see some young punk nigga trying to block the walkway toward the restrooms.

"C'mon, nigga. Bring her in here," another voice blared, coming from inside the men's restroom. "It's all clear."

"Mothafucka, you-better-let me-go," I heard again and I knew it was Lauren.

"See, I'm gonna fuck the shit outta this bitch here. Just watch."

"Let me go..."

I felt a mad adrenaline rush flow through my body when I realized the young-buck hovering over Lauren and who pushed her into the restroom was one of the young niggas that lived on my block.

I called out, "Dunkin?"

He stopped pushing and turned around to face me. "Who the fuck calling me?"

That's when I punched him in the jaw without hesitation. "What the fuck you do'n?"

"West?"

"Yeah, it's me. What the hell is this?"

"Man, we just fucking around. Don't worry—she 'wit us," he said.

I hit Dunkin in his jaw again and the fool he was with moved back further into the restroom away from Lauren.

"She's with me, nigga, and what the fuck you trying to do—rape her? You and your punk ass friend here are rapists, Dunkin?"

"That's exactly what he was trying to do. Punk ass nigga," Lauren said while she was adjusting her shirt.

Just the thought of this young boy trying to rape Lauren pissed me off. I had even fixed his mother's car once for free when she had no way to get his sorry ass back and forth when he was younger. Dunkin stood looking at me, wondering what I was going to do to him. There was no wonder he and his partner were up to no good. They both looked like two skinny punks, who were broke and would ask for your last dime any day of the week. I popped him in the jaw again.

"Damn it, West!"

"I should break it," I told him.

"Look, man, I didn't know she was your girl."

"I'm not his girl, nigga," Lauren said.

"And it don't matter. You out here trying to rape—I should beat you like she is my girl."

Dunkin said, "Aww, man, she was down 'wit it. She wanted to use a rubber. Said soon as we get in here she wanted to take it out her purse and strap it on me."

It happened so quick I didn't even see it coming—Lauren moved closer to Dunkin, snatched her handbag away from him and pulled out a pistol and told Dunkin to open his mouth and when he did, she told him, "No, nigga, this is what your ass was about to feel, bitch."

When Dunkin's boy saw the pistol he darted past me, and I slapped him in the back of the head. Dunkin called out for him not to leave him alone, but his punk ass was out of luck.

I gasped along with Dunkin when I heard Lauren pull the trigger on her snub-nosed 357; she was prepared to tear the young boy's mouth completely the hell up.

Lauren was heated.

"C'mon, Lauren. Fuck it. No harm, no foul," I said.

"Fuck that, West. You really believe that shit? This bastard was going to rape me."

"No, I don't believe that. But I know this punk nigga. Let me handle it, okay?"

Lauren was a bad little something standing there with that pistol in Dunkin's mouth. Lauren decided, "Yeah, okay. We got shit to do anyway." Then she took her pistol and bust Dunkin as hard as she could with it, in his nuts and walked away.

I pulled Dunkin back up. "Look, you stupid ass young nigga. The next time you might not be so lucky. You come by my shop—so you can make this up or I'm coming to look for your ass and you won't like it—you hear?"

Dunkin shook his head yes and I hit him in the jaw again and walked back to the car hoping we hadn't missed Rossi.

➤ ➤ ➤

Lauren was in the front seat munching on her popcorn when I got back to the car.

"So you're sure we're supposed to meet him here?"

"Yup." My eyes were on the screen.

"You two could have picked a new movie. I've already seen this."

"Turn around and look out the back window. *Jackie Brown* is playing on six. Pam Grier's the shit in that movie."

"I'll pass."

"Why not?"

"'Cause, I don't read lips."

"Well, can you be quiet so I can hear this movie? It's bad enough I have to listen to the sound of the movie from everybody else's car since you don't have FM frequency up in here."

Lauren offered me some popcorn.

"Can't stand it."

"No?"

"Nope. So where'd you get the gat?"

"Off the street. I live on the streets, have you forgotten?"

"You think you would have shot them niggas?"

"Oh, hell yeah, with outta doubt. I already had it made up in my mind I was going to blow his fucking brains out." Lauren paused. "My sister thinks I need to get rid of it though. She said this gun is making me crazy."

"Well, if you pull it, you gotta use it."

"Whatever."

"So how's your sister?"

"Don't wanna talk about her."

"You brought her up."

"Not talking about her ass though. You heard enough the other night anyway."

I reached down to finally have at my beer. "What's up with this warm ass beer?" I threw my can out the window.

"Wasn't warm when I got it."

"When was that?"

"Couple days ago."

I looked around the lot. "Where is this nigga?"

"Relax."

"Relax?"

"Yes. We have him right where we want him. Just remember the split has to be three ways—no more, no less."

"I told you fifty-fifty with Rossi, then down the middle with us." I was getting annoyed over the split discussion with Lauren.

"Whatever."

Right before Denzel shows his new partner his office in the movie, Lauren asked, "Have you thought about what you're going to do with your money yet?"

"Go'n to put it into my shop, fix up the place a bit. Maybe give a job or two to the brothers in the hood who can't find work—when I get a steady customer base. What about you?"

Lauren looked around her car a bit. "Get me a better car, for starters."

"What you gonna do with this?"

"I don't know? Take it someplace, take the license plate off, and then walk away from it."

"Oh, hell no, you won't. Let me have it. I'll have this piece of shit running like it's supposed to in no time. Have you forgotten, I need a car and you talk'n about throwing a mothafucka away."

"Okay. We get paid and it's yours."

I started to think about my stolen car again while Lauren whispered non-stop; she munched on her popcorn about how good Denzel Washington looked and how happy she was when he won the Oscar. I asked her if she thought about how we were going to get four more jurors to vote our way in the case.

She said, "I've thought about it and the only thing to do is to play the race card."

"Race card?"

"Yeah. Don't you read the papers; watch television; shit, read *Newsweek*, *Jet* or *Ebony*, Negro?"

"No."

"Well, shit, you ain't stupid, West. The race card is happening these days and it hasn't been an issue yet on the grand jury so I might as well bring it up."

"Lauren, I don't care how cool you think this mothafucka Rossi is. The nigga's white."

"But he has some black in him somewhere; I'm sure of it. This white boy has been raised in the hood. He talks black, acts black. Dresses nice. That's how we're gonna do it."

"Fuck me. This shit ain't gonna work," I told her.

"If you got any better ideas, let me know." Then Lauren got a burst of energy. "I know what we should do."

"What, what is it?"

"Let's just pass everybody a note and tell them what we're up to."

"Yeah, right."

"Look, there's two blacks; seven whites and three are women; one Latino and what's that old man?"

I didn't know. All I knew about his ass was that he looked Japanese or Thai or something—but we couldn't depend on him because he acted as though he didn't understand what was going on half the time, and he always voted with the majority. I told Lauren bottom line, we needed four more votes or our meeting with Rossi was going to be a waste of time. She told me not to be worried. But I was.

About ten minutes later I noticed our man Rossi walking slowly in front of the car. The second time he passed I had Lauren flash her parking lights. Rossi walked past us, then doubled back and tapped on the rear door window and sat in the back. He looked as though he was hot, so when he was settled I told him there was beer in the back.

"Thanks." He opened one, took a sip, then spit it out the window. "Shit's warm?"

"Oh, my bad." I turned to him. "Okay, let's deal, man."

Rossi swiped his brow and with a bitter brew face said, "Cool—let's do this."

"We want to split the three-hundred grand three ways. No more, no less. You got that?" Lauren looked at me surprised. I just had to get a better deal. Rossi looked nervous to me about jail so I went for it. "And when we're finished with this shit, I don't know you and you don't know us."

"Three ways?" Rossi repeated.

"That's right. It's a damn good deal considering you're getting your freedom without having to go to trial."

I turned around to look at Rossi in the back seat after he didn't respond. His eyes were fixed on Lauren, and I was about to break down to fifty-fifty but I held stern.

"You know, I forgot to tell you last night. You sure are fine, Lauren. Those braids really bring out your eyes. I bet you work out, don't you?" Lauren didn't turn around to respond. Her eyes shifted over to me after she smiled. I turned and looked at him. "Oh, my fault, dog," Rossi said. "I didn't know she was your girl."

"She's not, nigga," I told him. "Look, man, let's do this. Oh, yeah, there's something I wanted to tell you last night. You're piss'n everybody on the grand jury off with your long-winded statements and shit. Keep that shit to a minimum on Monday, okay?"

"Yeah, yeah. I'll try to remember. Three ways, that's your offer?"

"That's the deal; straight down the middle," I let him know again.

"Three ways, three ways, three ways of three hundred thousand," Rossi repeated. "Okay, yeah. That shit's fair. I just ain't the one to be doing no time. Forget that. Those guards are bound to have it out for me once they hear there's a chance I have some money on the outside waiting on me when I get out. Those bastards aren't throwing me in a cell with a bunch of horny ass brothers—no offense—but hell no. Time, I cannot do."

"Okay, after the vote, if things go well, where do you want to meet?" I asked him.

"Hold up. What do you mean *if?* You're going to work this out, right?"

"Don't worry," Lauren said, "We got you covered."

The car was silent. Gunshots from the movie brought us all back.

"Okay, one hour after the vote, I'll call you, West. Let me have your number."

We exchanged numbers on the napkins Lauren brought back from the snack stand.

Rossi opened the door and put one leg out of the car onto the gravel pavement.

I turned around and looked at him cold in the face. "Don't fuck us, Rossi. You think that beer was bitter, nigga. Fuck us, and you'll see some bitter shit. Trust that."

"Don't worry; you get me out this shit and I'll take care of you—both of you."

10

I caught the bus downtown Monday morning and that's when it hit me how much I really missed my car. Everything about the bus was lame. I never enjoyed being up against a bunch of mothafuckas I didn't know. Riding the bus was something I never did; not even when I first moved to Atlanta. I would at least take a cab. But my money was so tight that the bus was my only alternative; especially since it was a no-go to be seen with Lauren.

Without my wheels I was forced to get down to the Federal Building earlier than I had been making it and I caught all of the rush going inside. There were long lines waiting to get inside. Everyone who entered was required to go through a metal detector and have their bags searched. After the search I finally made it up to our room. As usual it was way too chilly inside. Most of the jurors were standing around chatting about their weekends. I overheard conversations about the Williams sisters playing tennis, burnt barbecue, and a corny joke about sex. I watched as the court clerk placed note pads on the table for the jurors' use. I reminded myself that those pads were basically the reason I was up to no good. Lauren and I decided it was a good idea for us not to talk, not even look at one another so we wouldn't draw attention to ourselves.

➤ ➤ ➤

I was sitting in my chair pretending to read my Sunday sports page while peeping the mood of the other jurors. Lauren stood in the hallway sipping on a cup of coffee. The one time we did make eye contact, she looked confused; like our plan wasn't going to work. I noticed the DA when he walked past Lauren in the hallway. His small choppy steps made me want to get up and bitch-slap his ass. There was a tall, husky black man walking behind him that I'd never seen before. At first glance, I thought he looked like the dude that played Linc in the original *Mod Squad*. His Afro was small with streaks of gray. He looked as though he had been chewing on the DA about something. The man made me nervous so on my way to the can, I moved close to him and had a chance to read his nametag. He was Captain Stallings of the Narcotics Division. The cop who Rossi claimed set him up and demanded he work in the sting.

When our session began the DA once again tried to remind everyone of the importance of jury service and the very difficult job associated with being on a grand jury. He went on a tangent talking some bullshit about in his opinion every case that came to the grand jury was good enough to go to trial. Once again he was trying to sway the jury. I became angry because it made me think about how many brothers this bastard had actually done wrong. As he continued, I began to feel good that I had a chance to fuck DA Anderson back and, if we succeeded, it was going to be like pouring a little liquor out for the brothers who were locked up for no damn good reason.

Rossi walked in with a strut and complete confidence. Before he took his seat in the middle of the jurors, he smoothed his tie neatly close to his body. I think he got that shit off television or something and thought he looked good doing it. Our seats were in a semicircle facing him. At that moment I didn't feel particularly good about the situation because everyone, for some reason, seemed to be so tense.

"Good morning, Mr. Rossi," DA Anderson said. Sarcasm was in the air.

Rossi blew him off. "If you say so. But I tell you one thing..."

"Which is?"

"Last night was even better." Rossi looked around at the jury after he heard a few snickers.

Anderson put an even tighter frown on his face and said, "We don't want to hear about last night, Mr. Rossi. We want to hear about the night when the Atlanta Narcotics Division employed you to bring down two notorious drug dealers and placed three-hundred thousand dollars in your hands for a transaction. Money that's nowhere to be found. Tell us about that."

"That's true," Rossi said. He was calm.

Anderson inquired, but was quick. "What's true?"

"That I had three-hundred thousand dollars in my possession working as a snitch for narcotics and after the bust, the money came up missing. It's true."

"Yes, it's true. And you have it, don't you?"

Rossi shook his head. "No, but I wish I did."

"Is that so? Tell me, Peter, what would you do with three-hundred thousand dollars?" Anderson started in with the name-calling.

"Shoot, I don't know…Purchase you some height, maybe?" The jurors thought it was a good joke.

Anderson's tightened face had reached its limit. "Mr. Rossi, as funny and lighthearted as you may think this is, don't you realize you're facing twenty-five years, maybe more because of your priors?"

"Yeah, and it bothers me," Rossi told Anderson.

"Why?"

"Because I don't have the money and I would be an innocent man locked up behind bars with no hope of getting out. That's a very scary thought, Mr. Anderson, but I'm sure you don't have those types of things to worry about."

I thought it was good that Rossi turned the tables on the asshole.

Anderson smiled. "You're right. I don't. But I do have to worry about low-lifes the police, for whatever reason, decide are capable of handling delicate street situations and turn around and…let's just say, stick it to the taxpayers."

I looked over at Captain Stallings. He looked a bit uncomfortable.

"Like I said all along, Anderson, I don't have the money," Rossi said.

"Rossi, have you ever stolen anything?"

"Not lately. And definitely not the three bills."

"That wasn't my question."

"Yeah, I have and you know that. I've done time as a juvee for breaking and entering."

"So you *would* take something that didn't belong to you?"

"I have before…yes. But not now—it was a phase."

"Tell us, how do you support yourself?"

"Look, man, I get by, okay. I work odd jobs. But all of a sudden your officers want to arrest me on some bogus charges and tell me they will go away if I do some work for free." Rossi nodded at Stallings. "Captain Stallings could take the stand and testify to that. He's the one who hired me."

Just then Stallings noticed that some of the jurors followed Rossi's eyes and looked him over, including me. When our pupils met, I looked in another direction.

The entire morning went back and forth. At one point Anderson went into Rossi's entire family history and pulled out everything he had on every single one who had a traceable crime history. But Rossi turned the tables on Anderson with his facial expressions to the jury, which infuriated Anderson. So, he broke for lunch for thirty minutes. I wasn't in the mood for lunch, and Lauren's wink and nod gave a brother the indication that she was ready. So I called Tammy.

"Hello?"

"Hey, baby. What're you doing?"

She said, "In bed relaxing. When are you coming home, West? You only have one case, right?"

"That's right."

"You gonna do it to me when you get here?"

"If things work out, I will. Hopefully, we're going to party tonight. If things don't work out, I gotta get in the shop as soon as I get in and make my money."

"Umm," Tammy moaned. "I can't wait to feel you up in me, West."

"Tammy?"

"Yes..."

"What you do'n?"

"Nothing, baby...Why you ask?"

I put my ear closer to the phone, and then looked around to make sure none of the nosey jurors were in my conversation. "'Cause it sounds like you hit'n it."

She said, "I'm not hittin' it, West. I'm just touchin' it."

"Touch'n it?"

"Umm, hmm. I'm going to let you *hit* it."

I had always been a freak so I wanted to see if I could make Tammy pop over the phone. "Do me a favor, baby."

"What is it? I'm so horny I'll do anything right about now."

"Stick..." Right when things were getting heated, I heard knocking at my door through the phone and my first thought was it was that nigga Todd. I had asked Tammy three times who the hell had the nerve to knock on my door so early in the afternoon and she pleaded that she didn't know. I was thinking if it was Todd, I was dropping everything and going home to teach him a lesson; fuck the grand jury and the money. Tammy sat the phone down to answer it but I could still hear everything going on.

"Yeah? Who is it?" Tammy asked through the door.

"It's Mr. Merrick. Mr. Merrick, the owner of the repair shop that I'm renting out to West."

"He's not here," Tammy told him.

"I can barely hear you!" Merrick shouted. He was an old man, I think in his eighties, who always wore suits and kept his outdated shoes spit-shined to the max. When I heard him through the phone, for the first time I was happy that I wasn't home 'cause I didn't have a dime to pay him for rent on my shop or the car I bought from him that was now stolen. I could hear Tammy open the squeaky front door, then the screen door slammed shut.

"West isn't here, Mr. Merrick."

"Not here, you say? Well, I'm renting him my old garage but it hasn't been open for days and I came by to see why. Plus, he owes me for the car."

"He's on jury duty."

"West?"

"That's right. And he hates it but today is his last day."

"All-righty then. I hope so, 'cause you know you can't make no payments if you don't work and he already owes me. Tell him to give me a call, okay?"

11

After lunch Rossi wasn't invited back in. It was time for the assistant DA to review the case to the grand jury. Her spiel lasted about forty-five minutes. When Allen finished, she asked the jury if we were unclear about any of the evidence. There were no questions so she left the room. The clerk opened up the floor for discussion and motioned to vote to send Rossi's case to trial.

Elliot, the most outspoken person on the jury, stood up: this guy was a jerk who didn't have a clue and always talked about how much money he had during the breaks. He usually wore a dress shirt, outdated tie and scuffed-up shoes with uneven heels. But for the last day of service he wore old faded blue jeans, penny loafers and a Yale sweatshirt. "Look guys, I think he's guilty and we've spent way too much time on this. If he doesn't have the money, who does? The DA has questioned him for two days and the only thing he's repeatedly said is he 'doesn't have it.' I mean, c'mon, what does he think we are, idiots?"

A few jurors nodded. The clerk was now in control of the jury because the DA was not allowed to address us. The clerk was a quiet man and well dressed, but I could tell he was Anderson's flunky. He looked around the room and waited a beat. "Anything else?" the clerk asked. No one answered. If there were no other concerns, the clerk would motion to vote. I moved my eyes to Lauren but she was already on her way to stand so she could address the jury. The room seemed to get extra quiet because it was the first time she'd ever stood concerning a case.

"Well, I don't think he has it." Lauren's tone was aggressive but very passionate. The tone of the room dimmed and Lauren noticed because she looked at everyone. "Well, I don't. How do we know for sure he has it? Yes, the money is gone but show me the evidence that shows he took the money. I haven't seen it and you know what? I think just because Mr. Rossi isn't like every other ordinary *white man*, the DA is trying to pin the missing money on him."

"What do you mean, 'ordinary white man'?" Elliot asked.

"Aww…come off it, Elliot. You know what I'm talking about." Lauren was good. Her performance was hyping me up. "If you were to hear his voice in a dark alley, you would swear he was a black man. Quite frankly, I don't think the DA likes that. For some reason he doesn't like the way Mr. Rossi speaks, sits or dresses. He just doesn't like it; he's entirely *too* black."

Elliot looked around at all the jurors like what Lauren had to say was all bullshit. "Look, he had the money and when it was time to give it back, he didn't. Case closed. Let's go home."

"Is it that simple?" Lauren questioned the jurors. "Elliot, you know what? I've been watching how you vote on all the cases. And you know what? You're as bad as the DA because you haven't voted on one case with an open mind. You've been looking at these people and voting on them on the basis of whether they look guilty or not; not if the evidence shows that they are."

Elliot pushed his finger toward Lauren. "You have no right to say that to me."

"Well, I said it. And you have," Lauren fired back.

"Come to think of it, Elliot, you have been rather quick to jump to conclusions. I think we need to hear her out," one of the white women on the jury said.

"Thank you, Helen. And I know everyone else in here can't truthfully say they know for sure that man took the money."

"That does seem to be the DA's only question," Helen added. "I began counting when I noticed his repetition of his questions and in the last

hour of questioning, he asked Mr. Rossi if he took the money, let's see…"
Helen looked at her note pad. "Over twenty-five times. Now if the DA
doesn't know for sure, how the hell can we?"

"Exactly," Lauren shot out.

"Oh, boy, I see hormones are raging this morning," Elliot lashed out.

"What?" Lauren asked.

"Excuse me?" Helen protested.

Elliot said, "You two are being typical women and you're reading between
the lines."

"Oh, so now we're *typical women*?" Lauren looked around. "Ladies, can
you believe this? We're now typical? Like I said before, Elliot, do you
have a problem with minorities or Mr. Rossi not being a typical *white*
man? As you and your warped vision should see him to be?"

Elliot looked at the clerk with his palms toward the ceiling, then
shouted, "That's outrageous!"

"No, it's not. You and the DA have a problem with him because he's not
typical and you want to stick it to him just like I've watched you stick it
to every other person who's been brought in here without sufficient
evidence. We should all report ourselves because we've let it happen,"
Lauren charged.

All of a sudden a nervous-looking white man stood up. Homeboy
looked soft. I don't even remember him ever clearing his throat. He said,
"Well, I have to say, there have been a few times last week when I wasn't
quite sure whether or not a couple of those drug dealer guys were found
with drugs on them." His tone was nasal and he seemed shy. He stood
with his hands in his pockets. "I kind of believed them when they said
they 'didn't have drugs on them and the police planted it on them by
throwing it at their feet when they were approached.' But after the speech
the DA gave every morning about all the lies defendants tell so they don't
have to go to trial, I just dismissed what they were telling us as a lie and
voted for their cases to go to trial."

"Thank you, Harry," Lauren said. "See, that's what I mean. We've all
done it. Today is the day for us to stop judging the people sitting in that

chair and judge the damn evidence because the DA and Elliot or anybody else shouldn't be able to lead our decisions. We're talking about people's lives here," Lauren reminded the jury.

The clerk stood up. "Hold on one second," he said. "Just hold on." He walked out of the room into the hallway. My seat was closest to the door and I could see the DA and Captain Stallings approach the clerk. I got up and stood by the water cooler to see if I could hear them but I couldn't. After a few minutes the clerk returned and stood at his desk holding a cup of water. Most of the jurors didn't notice him when he reentered because they were talking amongst themselves about what had transpired. I figured he told Stallings and Anderson what was going on with the jury. No one said anything to me during the break, which was normal.

"Okay, are we ready?" the clerk asked. "I'm sorry about that. I felt myself about to continue with this terrible cough I picked up and to prevent from embarrassing myself and at the same time grossing you all out, I decided to gag outside instead." He gave us all a fake ass smile.

"Anyway, I'm ready to vote," Elliot demanded. "Anybody else ready in here?" Three of Elliot's cronies nodded "yes."

I looked around the room. I knew that Elliot's running mates were ready to vote "bill" and send Rossi to trial. Somehow that loyalty needed to be broken. From day one, the group formed and became an overpowering clique. They laughed together, even went out to lunch and dinner afterwards together as a pack and didn't care who knew.

Fuck that shit. I rose up from my seat and it drew everyone's attention. "I have something to say before we vote," I told them all.

"The floor is yours," the clerk let everyone know.

"When I was growing up and still, to this day, my worst fear in life has been going to prison. I've never been, but I would imagine it wouldn't be the best place to be; especially if you've done nothing wrong."

"What the hell is this?" Elliot asked.

I shot Elliot a hard look, letting him know I would break his freak'n neck if he didn't let me finish, and he backed off. "So, when we vote and decide to send Mr. Rossi to trial, so another jury can once again decide on his innocence or guilt, you have to look at it and realize they're going to look at our decision here today. If the vote is taken and he's sent to trial, that means the next jury will think, we all think, he's guilty even though they'll be told that we have only found enough *evidence* to send him to trial, which would be a lie. I can just see the DA working his spin on that one. Now I don't know about anyone else sitting in this room, but I don't want to send a man to a jury trial with the possibility of going to prison when the evidence doesn't show he's done anything wrong. Respectfully, I have to say some of the people in this room have been very biased, and I've noticed it when we take our votes and when I walk in here every day—for the last week for that matter."

Elliot just wouldn't shut the fuck up. "What're you talking about?"

"I'm talking about how everyone in your little clique over there seems so quick to judge."

Elliot looked around with a smirk. "That's what we're here for, right, fellows?"

I interrupted their laughter. "But you didn't come here to judge me, did you?"

Elliot exhaled. "What are you saying?"

"I just want to know the reason no one over there on your side of the room nor you has said one thing to me in over a week, even when I tried to be sociable to every last one of you—especially you, Elliot."

"You've never said one word to me," Elliot said.

He was right. Personally, I thought he was a punk bitch, but the other jurors would never know. It was war. So I continued. "Not one *good morning*, not one *how's it going*, not even one *kiss my ass*. Just silence and glances as though I threaten you. And I wonder if it's the same way you've looked at all the people who've been before us who I know for sure you definitely can't relate to because ninety-nine percent of them looked just like me." And that was the fucking truth. The DA was running niggas in and out of our sight on charges all week.

Elliot and his crew looked at one another. Then Melisa stood up. She was one of the three white women on the grand jury. She looked to be in her late-twenties. "You know, West is right. You guys huddled over there sure have been a bunch of pricks. Ever since you found out I wasn't going to stand for your little sexual jokes and crude comments the very first day of duty, not one of you has said 'Hells Bells' to me." Melisa started to sit back down when she noticed everyone's eyes on her. She looked around. "I mean it."

The clerk stepped in right on cue. "Does anyone need to hear any more testimony read back?"

In unison everyone shouted, "No!"

It was time to vote.

12

Lauren was so hyped that it didn't seem to matter that her muffler slipped down another few inches and was scraping the pavement as we drove down the street after jury duty was over.

"We did it, West. I knew we could pull it off. Did you see the DA's eyes looking at the jury when he came in to thank us for serving? He was one sick puppy."

"Now he was carrying a load, wasn't he?"

"All up in his pants," Lauren joked. "Now all we need to do is get to your place and wait on the phone call to get paid. You think he's going to call?"

"Said he would." I was about eighty-five percent sure he would, but there was the other fifteen percent. "You ever bought something from someone off the street?"

"Bunch of times, why?"

"'Cause that's as much as we can trust Rossi right now."

"Well, I'm going to trust him."

"We don't have a choice."

I don't know why, but a brief moment of silence passed and a thought of Todd was able to creep into my mind; *the nerve of that nigga bringing food into my house.*

"What's wrong with you, West? I thought you'd be running alongside the car by now with a big smile plastered on your chubby face."

"Don't think a brother ain't going to celebrate. Something just shot through my mind."

"Really? Right now?"

"Yeah, some real ignorance."

"Like what? What could be on your mind right now besides our money?"

"Tammy."

"Tammy?"

"The other day some buster brought over a bunch of groceries and whatnot—and had the nerve to be sit'n up in my place like he was 'bout to move in."

"Get out of here!"

"It was about to get ugly up in there—and that's my word."

"So—what did Tammy have to say about the little situation?"

"She was like, 'he's a friend.' Friend-my-ass. Men just don't do that type of thing, Lauren. I should've beat him down, 'cause now—I look soft. I let this bastard leave without putting a dent in his head. Now he probably thinks I'm cool with it, even though I told him I wasn't—and that to me looks soft."

"West, you-are-not-soft. Don't worry about it. Maybe he really is her friend and wanted to help out. There *are* guys like that, ya' know."

"Like who?"

"You're nice."

"Yeah, but you just don't walk into another Negro's house with groceries without getting clearance first. That is straight-up disrespectful. Plus, if it was me, I ain't buying no groceries if I'm not fuck'n and that's on the strength right there."

"Oh, so you wouldn't buy a woman groceries if you weren't going to bed with her?" Lauren prodded.

"Not even for Mother's Day. No—I wouldn't do it. Hell no, that ain't in my handbook."

"Player handbook, right?"

"You know all about it, don't you?"

"Every guy has one, don't they?"

"Unh, unh, they're only for players."

"Well, give him the benefit of the doubt. Let the man slide this time.

Plus, in a few hours you're going to have enough money to buy plenty of groceries."

Lauren made a left-hand turn and her muffler sounded like it had dropped down even more but she didn't care. She said when she got her money, in her hand—her car was history.

"You know you surprised me back there today," Lauren told me.

"I got acting skills, too," I told her. "I was all up in high school drama class. Reading Langston, DuBois, making people feel something."

"Negro, stop fronting. West, you know some of that shit you said back there was from the heart. You don't have to admit to it. But I know it was."

"Okay, I give you that. At least a bit of it—especially about going to jail. But ain't it kinda screwy we're gonna use the outcome for our own benefit?"

"Forget…that. I'm not thinking about it like that. The whole system is screwed-up. The police tried to use money to entrap the guys in the first place. I've been thinking 'bout it too, and if they didn't give Rossi the money to present it to his connections in the first place, a deal wouldn't have been going down. People move when there's money thrown in their face. We're examples of that. Just as long as we don't blow this chance to make good of our lives, then I don't have a problem with what we did."

"Don't get it twisted. I didn't say I felt bad for doing it. I need to get paid, damn it. I'm using this bad money for good."

"Yeah, I like that. 'Cause I found out that's exactly what I'm going to have to use my money for."

"What you mean by that?"

"Found out I was pregnant last night."

"Pregnant?"

"That's right. I'm having a baby, West. After all the shit I've been telling my sister about being careful, look what happens to me."

I started to light up a smoke but I thought of the baby and put it back in my shirt pocket. Then I wondered who the father of the baby was since Lauren had never mentioned even being involved with anyone.

"Some guy. Is that what you're thinking, West—that's who."

"I know it has to be a guy—what do I look like here. But who is he?"

"I really don't know him—that's the problem. It was just one night and he doesn't even know yet. I went out with him a couple of times and decided to give him some on a whim. He works at JDS in a management position and now that I'm pregnant I need this money to get my kid off to a good start in life and to stop living in this dirty ass car—get off these streets."

"You gonna tell him you knocked up?"

"I don't know; I don't even like his ass."

"So what?'

"So, this is my baby."

"Your baby?"

"That's right."

We drove a few more blocks, both thinking about her situation—and it didn't damper our mood because we were about to get paid our money. I turned to her. "A baby, hunh?"

"A baby," Lauren confirmed.

13

My place was quiet when we arrived. I wanted Tammy to be there so I could fill her in on what went down, but she was nowhere to be found. Lauren copped a spot on the couch. I went to the fridge—for a beer and apple juice for Lauren. There was a note on the fridge. It was from Tammy; she let me know she had gone over to her family's house. I just knew it was to break up another family fight. Twenty minutes later, the phone rang.

"West?"

"Speak'n."

"It's Rossi. Good job…my man. Damn good job. Is Lauren there with you?"

"She's here."

"Give her my thanks."

"Done. When we gonna meet?"

"Tonight. How about at the strip joint. I'll have a table ready for you in VIP. Let's say about eleven?"

"We'll be there."

➤ ➤ ➤

Lauren woke me up around ten. She was changed and ready to go. She must have had a gang of clothes in the trunk of her car because, once again, homegirl looked good. She even looked better than the first time I saw her when she cleaned up. I followed suit and put on a nice pair of black slacks, a white button-down and my black derby with a big fat cigar dangling from my lip. Lauren thought it was a damn joke when I told her I was ready to hit the club. She didn't understand the straight-up old-school pimping style I was brought up on. My uncles taught a brother right. When I was coming up—hats meant something. Meant you had class and at the same time didn't take any shit like Walt Frazier and those fur coat-wearing niggas who used to play with the New York Knicks.

It wasn't until we were a few minutes from the club that I realized I hadn't spoken to Tammy—but it was too late to stress over. I had to be on my game to make sure things would run smoothly with our money—it was not every day a brother and sister got handed one-hundred grand each.

> ➤ ➤ ➤

When we stepped in the club, things looked as though they were going to work out. The atmosphere was even fiercer than the first time we visited. The DJ was ripping wicked mixed rap beats over some Mary J. Blige and the girls working the pole were giving it their all. We moved through the club and straight for VIP where Rossi said he would meet us. Once inside our names were on a card sitting on a table with a bottle of bubbly on ice.

"So, we gonna split right after we get the money or what?" Lauren asked.

"Let's play it by ear and let me know if you see anyone walk'n with him."

"If so, then what?"

"Don't worry about it. I just want to make sure he's alone."

Passion came up to the table. "Hey guys! Guess who's working VIP tonight! The boss says keep the bubbly flowing all night for you two— and that's exactly what I'm gonna do. I always knew you were somebody important." Passion looked directly at Lauren. "Girl, I've been waiting on my phone call." Lauren smiled and played Passion off as best she could without disrespecting her, then mentioned that she had been really busy but still had her number. I reached for a glass, then asked Passion to bring some juice out for Lauren. Passion switched away.

Lauren said, "You sure are concerned with me drinking my juice."

"Somebody needs to be."

"What's that supposed to mean?"

"Just what I said. You got a life in there. You gotta make sure you feed it right."

Lauren stood up. "Okay, you get my juice and I'll be back 'cause I have to go pee."

Passion came back with Lauren's juice and shot me a really freaky look. She saw that my glass was half empty and she picked up the bottle of champagne and when she bent over the table to pour, her tits fell from her negligee and I couldn't help to look at them as they jiggled in my face. When Passion strutted away, I took some time to relax with my drink and cigar—watching the girls do their thing.

Lauren plopped back down in her seat. There was no guessing that she was pissed off about something.

"I can't believe it," she said.

"What?"

"Lex."

"Lex?"

"Yeah, my sister."

"What about her?"

"She's out there humpin' on that brass pole."

"Are you sure?"

"Yes, I'm sure, nigga. I can recognize my sister when I see her—even through all those damn blazing lights."

"Well, you told her to get off the streets, didn't you?"

"Yeah, but..."

"At least she's in here where it's safe."

"I guess."

"So how's she doing out there? She work'n it or what?"

"Fuck you, West."

I smiled at Lauren and threw my glass back again.

"She said she's off in a few hours. She asked me to take her to her room afterwards."

"Cool with me. After Rossi comes in here and gives us our money, all I will have is time. Time to do whatever the hell I like."

14

Lex and Passion joined us in our booth about two hours later. There was no sign of Rossi and it was damn near one-fifteen in the morning. Passion had been sitting between Lauren and me on and off and telling us tricks of the trade as Lex soaked up her experience working in the club. I wasn't interested in how Passion made it from humping the brass pole to her promotion of walking around butt naked in VIP—giving at least two blowjobs a night to big spenders for over five hundred dollars a pop. I asked Passion for the phone and reached in my pocket for Rossi's number. There was no answer. We waited another hour or so but he never showed so we decided to leave.

Once again, Lauren became upset with Lex after she found out Lex left her son Lil'Man with some dope fiend named Preach. Lex swore he didn't use anymore, and her son was safe. But Lauren didn't believe her and as far as I could tell, Lauren didn't like Preach at all. We had to drive out to *Little Five Points* and at this point all I wanted to do was get home and forget about the whole night and our scam because I was pissed that we didn't get our money from Rossi.

"Okay, ya'll wait here," Lex told us.

For what reason we had to park in an alley was beyond me. I sat up from my slouched position in Lauren's car though: I didn't like the idea of being in a damn alley in the first place around two in the morning. About five minutes later, Lex came back to the car with tears streaming down her face.

She said, "Preach's roommate said he took Lil'Man out about three hours ago and he ain't seen him since." The cracking of Lex's voice told me she was scared to no end.

"What do you mean?" Lauren said.

"Just what I said. He ain't up there with my son and he got him out in the street somewhere?"

Lauren opened the car door and got out. "I told you not to ever leave the baby with that fool again."

Lex said, "So what we going to do?"

"We 'bout to find my nephew, that's what," Lauren told her. When Lauren shut the door, there was a voice, followed by an echo calling out from the alley.

"Hey, Lex…that you? Lex…Lex, it's me, Preach."

"That fool is out here in the alley," Lauren said. "West, we'll be back."

"Well, ya'll hurry up 'cause I don't like sit'n out here like this."

I watched them walk to the end of the alley. It was about sixty-to-seventy feet away. At the end of the alley was a wall that was connected to an apartment building. I couldn't see much but I figured Preach was sitting on the ground because Lauren and Lex were looking down. I didn't like the look of things so I turned on the headlights of the car, then got out and sat on the hood and lit up a smoke.

"Where's Lil'Man?" Lex asked him.

"You got my money?" Preach wanted to know. By the sound of his voice I knew he was fucked-up off something.

"What the hell you talking about, Preach?" Lex said. "You know I'll straighten you out as soon as I can. Now where's my son?"

"Fuck your son. I want my money, bitch."

"Nigga, what the hell you talking about?" Lauren said. "I tell you what—you better tell us where he is or you're getting beat down and I mean it."

Preach snapped back. "I ain't got 'em, bitch."

Lex put her hand over her mouth, and then began to shake as though she was cold but I knew she was scared.

"Where is he, Preach?" Lauren asked again.

"Fuck you, bitch," he shot back.

Lauren didn't waste any time. She jumped down on Preach and they were on the ground struggling as Lex stood there crying out for her son. I didn't want to get on the ground scuffling with no stank crackhead, but Lauren was pregnant and I had to do something. So, I went to the car, pulled Lauren's gat from her purse and walked over to the commotion.

I pulled them apart. "Hold up, Lauren," I said.

"Yeah, bitch, hold up. Get the fuck off me," Preach instructed.

I looked down at Preach and he *was* fucked up. He smelled terrible and looked even worse. Preach was a skinny, brown-skinned Negro, with bulging eyes, smoked out gray lips and he had on a filthy white shirt with holes in his jeans while his hair hadn't been combed in weeks.

"Where's my son, nigga!" Lex shouted. "I can't believe you high, Preach. You punk nigga."

His speech was slurred. "Yeah, I'm high. So what? Give me my money and you get 'em back."

I said to the crackhead, "Look, how much she owe you?"

Preach rolled his eyes in the back of his head as though he was adding, but that fool probably couldn't even spell his own name. He raised one finger and said, "'Bout seven-hundred."

"You a damn lie!" Lex shouted.

Preach looked at Lex, then put up four fingers. "But I'll take two," Preach decided.

"Aight, cool." I pulled out a wad of ones that I had in my pocket that I was going to use as I celebrated our big score at the strip club and showed it to Preach. "Look, I got all that right here, then some," I let him know.

Preach held out his hand. "Give it to me den. C'mon, let me have the shit."

I said, "Unh, unh...where's the boy at?"

"Oh, it's like that?"

"That's the way it's got to be," I let him know.

Preach pointed. "He right over there. Right there under those boxes wrapped up."

Lex and Lauren ran over to him.

"You punk ass nigga," Lauren shot out.

"Yeah, whatever..."Preach said back.

Lauren and Lex were looking down at Lil'Man; afraid to pick him up.

"The little nigga ain't dead; his ass is sleep," Preach told them.

I asked Lauren and Lex if he was okay and they said yes. I told them to get back in the car and to pull the car out of the alley and onto the street. Seconds later, I was looking at Preach through the darkness, but I knew exactly where he was because I could see his white sneakers and still smell him just the same.

"So give me my money, nigga," Preach demanded.

"Say what?"

"Nigga, I said, I want my money."

"Fuck you. You ain't getting shit with your punk ass out here getting high when you supposed to be watching Lil'Man. I bet your mama real proud of your punk ass, ain't she?"

"Man...forget you. You lucky I ain't sell the bitch ass little boy like I was fix 'n to."

"You were going to do what?"

"You heard me and maybe the next time I will," he promised.

At the moment I felt like I was doing the right thing. I pulled the hammer back on the pistol and shot into the darkness. Preach wasn't running his mouth anymore, but he sure was screaming and crying like a baby though.

15

Lex kept her eyes peeled on me from the back seat while she held onto her son. I could tell she was wondering if I killed Preach or not. I didn't care if he was dead. I was feeling cold and without a conscious. I did wonder though if anyone saw me in the alley when I pulled the trigger. But there was no way they could; it was too damn dark—I hoped.

I blamed Preach for getting his ass shot; talk about selling a baby to me was sacrilegious and I blamed Rossi for my attitude. He played us and now I was still broke and my dreams of the money and what it could have been used for were nothing but a dream. I knew going in that it was a possibility of getting played by Rossi. But I thought just maybe he would do right by us—but we went to bed with a hustling devil and liar. Getting fucked was in the equation dealing with Rossi somewhere down the line.

When we arrived at my place, Lauren looked to be in shock. Getting done for our money and knowing I shot Preach—not to mention she was holding a baby—looked like it all was wearing her down very quickly. I would have invited her family inside for the night, but I didn't want to hear any shit from Tammy. However I did let them pull the car into my garage. It was heated and there was a couch in my office. They would be fine.

When they all were settled, I went inside. Tammy still wasn't there. I put down shot after shot of whiskey while thinking about the entire night and how those hot shells must have felt going up inside Preach. I had never shot a man before and just the thought of what I did forced me to drink more whiskey.

I fell asleep on my kitchen floor and woke up at the sound of pounding at my front door. It had to be close to six in the morning. I thought Tammy had forgotten her key. I peeped through the window, and then shook my head to get my focus. Son of a bitch; Captain Stallings was standing on the other side of the door holding his police badge. What the fuck did he want? I didn't know if I should run out the back door through the kitchen and down the stairs or open the door and confess every single detail about the shit we pulled on jury duty in exchange for a lesser charge and sentence. I was not doing time. I opened the door slowly as I wiped my mouth.

Stallings looked very demanding in front of the rising blinding sun.

"You West Owens?" he hammered. It took me much too long to answer him. I finally mumbled that I was. Stallings looked inside, then walked right past me. "Can I come in?"

I shut the door. Shit, all of a sudden everything that seemed so little to me seemed as though it was way too much to lose. I was one second from breaking down and asking for a deal like they do on all those television series. I really didn't like the way he was looking around my crib. Picking up my belongings and putting them back down wherever the hell he felt. There was no way that I was going to challenge him about it. He finally stopped meddling with my things, then turned to me.

"Do you know Tammy Hill?"

I wondered if he noticed when I exhaled because I was expecting him to say something about the jury, then I wondered. "What? Tammy?"

"Yeah. Does she live here?" Stallings began looking around again.

"Yeah? She lives here, but she didn't come home last night."

"Where were you last night?"

"Me? I went out."

"Out where?"

"To a strip joint downtown."

"By yourself?"

"Unh, unh, with a friend. What's this all about?"

"Shut the fuck up; I'll ask the questions. What's your friend's name?"

"Lauren."

"Lauren what?"

"Shit, I don't know. She never told me her last name."

"Is she a stripper?"

"Unh, unh, a friend."

"And you don't know her last name?" I shook my head no. "Anyone in the club can prove you were there?"

"Yeah, a dancer. Her name is Passion. She worked VIP all night. So what's this all about?"

"Tammy's dead," Stallings said.

"Dead? What the fuck are you talking about?"

"She's dead. Found her this morning on Bankhead Highway face down in a puddle of mud. She'd been strangled to death."

"Strangled? What the hell is going on?"

"That's what I'm trying to find out," Stallings said. Then he looked at me oddly. "Have we met before?" I told him "no" and asked him if there was anything else I could do for him.

Stallings left about ten minutes later and I was damn near in a state of panic. I thought maybe he made the whole thing up and it was part of his game of trying to start some shit because he found out about our plan with Rossi. My fucking head was spinning out of control. *Tammy dead? Gone? How? Who did it? For what reason? Did she suffer? Did she call for me? What the hell was going on?* I didn't know what to believe but as long as we'd been together she never had stayed out the entire night, so maybe what he had told me was true. I went to the garage to tell Lauren what was going on. I went out through the back door, then down the steps to the garage. She was already up, listening to the radio and making a pot of coffee in the waiting area.

She looked at me oddly. "You okay?"

I went to the front of the garage to see if any police cars were out front. On the way I could see Lex and Lil'Man under the covers huddled up in the back seat of Lauren's car sleeping. Lauren followed me and I moved her behind me with one arm.

"West, what's wrong?"

"Captain Stallings came over this morning."

"Captain Stallings?"

"Yeah, the cop that worked with Rossi on the drug bust. And what the fuck is your last name?"

"Nigga, what?"

"What is it, damn it?"

"Richards, nigga, why?"

"Stallings asked me."

"He asked about me and came over here?" Lauren stood on her tiptoes and tried to see over me.

"Get back. He just left the apartment."

"For what, West?"

"Tammy's dead."

"What?"

After I was sure Stallings had left, I went over to the coffeepot, picked up a cup and placed it under the drip spout before it was finished and burnt my hand.

"Are you sure? How could she be dead?"

"He said she was strangled to death. But I don't know if I should believe him or not. Maybe they're just holding her because they found out about the shit we did on jury duty."

"How the hell would they have found out?"

"We're talk'n about the poe-poe, Lauren. Those bastards are scandalous. Maybe Rossi told them."

"Rossi? So what we gonna do?"

"Gotta find out if he's lying or not."

"How?"

"I don't know."

Lauren suggested, "Let's call the morgue to find out."

"I got one better. Let's go down there to see ourselves."

➤ ➤ ➤

Captain Stallings wasn't the lying son of a bitch I thought he was. Tammy was dead. When Lauren and I made it to the morgue, I spotted her family and they were on me with burning eyes. They wanted my head; especially after seeing Lauren standing by my side. There was nothing I could tell them that would soothe their pain. They didn't believe that I was grieving, too, and they wanted to go to blows. I left the morgue after I saw Stallings peering at me during the commotion. I was sure I would see his ass again.

➤ ➤ ➤

And I was right. No sooner than I stepped back into my place, Stallings was knocking on my door with handcuffs in tow. He never said I was under arrest for Tammy's murder. He just forced me to turn around, slapped on the bracelets, and then threw me in the back seat of his car. I wasn't about to sit in the back seat with my hands behind my back and begin to talk shit to him, so I kept my black ass quiet. Once we got down to the station he pushed me into interview room number one, told me to sit down, then slammed the iron-cast door behind him. There was no reason why Stallings had to put my cuffs on so tight. They were cutting into my skin. The clock on the wall let me know that my circulation in my hands and arms had been cut off for more than ninety minutes, and I wanted to get up and look through the small square window in the door. But I can't lie; I was scared to move.

Finally, an officer came in and told me to stand up. He grabbed me by the arm and the next thing I knew the cuffs came off both my wrists. I was rushed down the hall and automatically cuffed again, this time one arm only, and connected to a bunch of fools in orange jumpsuits and flip-flops. I was plopped down in the first row of seats in a waiting room that looked to have five rows and seven seats wide. It was quiet inside the room and when the officer checked my cuff for a third time, he turned around and walked out. As soon as the door shut, a young nigga in the back hollered out and called the officer a pussy and the door was swung back open.

"All right, damn it. I told ya'll to keep your mouths shut. Don't let me hear some mo shit 'cause if I have to—I'll beat everybody's ass in here 'til you tell me who got the big mouth. Then I'm going to make that pussy suck on this nightstick dangling on my waist. Now shut the fuck up."

About thirty minutes later, the cuffs were off again and they strolled me in to see the judge on duty. I already knew he was in a bad mood because when some of the other men came back from being arraigned they were pissed at either the bond he set or where he sent them back to after they had been caught for doing some more stupid shit on the street. He asked me my name, then looked around on his desk for some type of file on me. He was angry that there was nothing. Then Captain Stallings cleared his throat and gave the judge the wink and nod. And the next thing I knew I was in a holding cell with at least thirty other fucked-up niggas with a five hundred dollar bail over my head.

There was only one phone inside the holding cell and I sat right next to it and called Lauren. I called my shop maybe twenty times before Lauren decided to pick it up.

"Hello? West Auto Repair Shop."

"Lauren?"

"West?"

"Yeah, it's me. Listen, Stallings brought me downtown to the station."

"I know, West. I saw him put you in the car. Are you all right?"

"Yeah, I'm all right, but I gotta get the hell outta here."

"Why did Stallings take you down?"

"He didn't say. I think he's just messing with me, 'cause if they would have charged me with Tammy's death, do you think they would have set my bail at five-hundred dollars?"

"I don't like Stallings, that punk."

"That makes two of us."

"So you got any money around here that I can bring to you?"

"Not a damn dime."

"Nothing, West?"

"I told you I was broke."

"Well, let me think of something and I will be down there to get you out. Just be patient, okay?"

"Lauren, just hurry up. This place is getting to me already."

$$\succ \; \succ \; \succ$$

I always knew jail wasn't for me and being up in that cell made me realize why. First of all, most of the assholes in there had been locked up before and they adjusted well inside. They ate the food, did the time with experience and fucked with the guards while having fun at just the same. For me, the whole place was disgusting. It smelled terrible, everybody wanted to know what the hell everyone else was in for, and the young punks inside talked too much for their own good. At least the holding cell was big enough where everyone had their own space and we weren't on top of each other. There were even two guys who paced the floor in the area where I sat and talked about how they needed to make bail so that they could make it to a huge drug-dealer gathering that was going to be held in a hotel downtown.

I sat in the holding cell about three more hours before I heard my name being called. When I went over to see what the guard wanted, he opened the cell, took me to processing and led me out to the lobby where Lauren and Lex were waiting for me.

"Free at last..." Lauren said.

Lex smiled.

"Damn, that was quick. What'd you do, jack a bank?"

Lauren looked at Lex. "Nope, Lex made some money."

"Not just some money, a thousand bills," Lex said.

"A thousand bills? Doing what?"

"Doing what I do," she said.

"I have to admit, she was working it," Lauren joked.

"Hold up. You sold...you know what to get me outta here?"

"Sure did."

"Damn, Lex, I dunno what to say."

"Then don't, let's just get outta here, before I see one of my police tricks."

16

Three months later

Atlanta needed rain and I more than ever was lacking money in my pockets. Over the past couple of months, we were all forced to watch the president run the table in the news with all his foreign policy and nation building; while at the same time, blow our minds telling us he didn't think the country was in a recession and all we needed to do was kick Iraq's ass and things would be fine. I wasn't listening to all the president's bull about the amount of money flowing where the majority of blacks lived because since he'd been in office—I'd never seen him even visit the hood.

I had firsthand knowledge of the economy in my community because hardly anyone had money to pay me to fix their automobiles. I was fed up with people coming in my shop trying to get work on credit. There wasn't going to be any of that. I had to eat, too, and walking into my place of business without any dough was definitely a no-go; I didn't care if someone came in holding their engine, cradled in their arms like an infant—it wasn't going to happen.

My hat was off to Mrs. Shirley Bullock though. She was doing a fine job keeping me in business and food on my plate on a regular basis. Her car was just about the only one I worked on steady and I was the reason for her car problems. I wasn't proud of that fact, but I made work for myself at her expense so I could eat.

One day she stopped by the shop complaining about her car's gas mileage, and I punched holes in the radiator and fucked up the timing a bit—to make sure she would come back and see me in a matter of days. Shit worked like a charm and I charged her out the ass for it, too. One thing about Mrs. Bullock: She loved her car and always paid me extra when I returned it running smooth. I didn't like to get over on her, but hell, she paid in cash.

Stallings had called me into his office twice since Tammy's death. He kept reminding me of my few hours of jail time and told me the next time I went in—it was going to be for years and more than likely life. He wasn't much of an interrogator. He seemed to have brain lapses, always forgetting his train of thought. He would forget questions he would ask but then again, I thought it could have been part of his game plan to make me spew out something that I'd never told him before. So I stayed steady and gave him the same answer over and over again no matter how forgetful he seemed. I told him hundreds of times that I didn't want Tammy dead. That was the truth. What we had was a deep understanding. She was mine and I was hers. I did for her; she did for me. Stallings let it slip while he was all up in my face with his coffee breath that he was placed in homicide because of a case he botched. I kind of guessed it was Rossi's case and it made me nervous to even think I was the reason for this limp-dick bastard now breathing down my back and watching my every move. Through our hours of questioning, Stallings never realized I was on the jury that set Rossi free and I damn sure wasn't going to volunteer the information.

> > >

Lauren and Lex never did leave my garage after Rossi stiffed us for the money and I found out that Tammy had been murdered. Lex, Lauren and Lil'Man all moved in with me. There was just no freaking way I was going to let them live on the streets with a two-year-old baby and another on the way—especially after what Lex did to get my ass out of jail. Lauren found work in a mom-and-pop diner around the corner and would bring home as much leftovers as she could carry every night while Lex continued to do what she did. The girls moved into my spare bedroom. Lauren didn't look pregnant, but in the mornings, I sure knew she was because she spent so much time in the bathroom throwing up.

17

Finally rain drenched the city. I opened up the front door and enjoyed the breeze blasting through the screen in the storm door while the rain cooled things down. I was pretty much used to Lauren and Lex at this point. Lil'Man took some time though, but he quickly grew on me and one of the things I kind of looked forward to when I came in from the garage was holding Lil'Man and blowing huge bubbles with my gum, which drove him crazy. Lauren was sitting on the couch next to me and she picked up a picture of Tammy that sat on my table next to the couch.

"You really loved her, didn't you?"

"I did, but I didn't—you know? But now that she's gone, I love what we had," I answered.

"Unh-unh, you can't love but not love, West."

"I'm telling you, that's how I felt."

"Why'd you love what you two had and not her?"

Lauren was smooth. Not once had we ever discussed Tammy in detail, and I enjoyed the fact that she never did bring her up because it was hard to even think about Tammy being murdered.

"I guess because I was used to her, used to what we had. Sometimes you get used to people, that's all. She was real. When I first met Tammy she was working as a nurse down at Crawford Long. I was downtown in a sandwich shop and was hungry as hell and ordered one of those big ass New York-style deli sandwiches. You know the ones with all that turkey on wheat with lots of mayo, tomatoes and lettuce with a bag of corn chips on the side and a Snapple to wash it all down?"

"You're making me hungry, West."

"Well, they fixed the sandwich up just like I like it; I could see it on the plate with my mouth watering and 'thangs—and when it came time for me to pay, I reached into my pocket and only had fifty cents to my name. Now fuck me…because it was an embarrassing moment—you hear."

"Oh hell naa…?"

"I ain't ly'n. Even the bag of chips cost more than I had in my pocket. But right before I had to be the 'nigga at the register who couldn't pay for his shit' in front of a gang of people, Tammy slid some money to the cashier and squashed the embarrassment right there. So I asked her to sit down with me and we kicked it from there."

"Aww, that's kinda sweet, West."

"It's not always about looks, you know?" I looked at Tammy's picture. She was definitely a round-the-way girl.

"I think she was nice-looking."

"Yeah, she fit right in with her lifestyle. See, with me, it's never been about looks. It's about how a nigga gets treated. Even though I didn't like and couldn't figure out what the hell she was doing with that nigga Todd, all of a sudden—she was still my girl and I tried to respect what we had without getting ugly." I noticed Lauren wipe her eyes. "Yo, what's up with you, Lauren?"

"It's my hormones, West."

"What about 'em? You all right?"

"Yeah, but every time I hear something sweet or nice I just start crying."

"Since when?"

"Started this week."

"So how long does this cry on a dime shit last?"

She looked up at me after she wiped her tears. "Nigga, I don't know. I ain't never been pregnant."

"Oh, so the baby is doin' this?"

Lauren started to laugh a bit, "Negro, don't you know anything about babies?"

"You see any around here?"

"Well, pregnant women cry when they get emotional, West. I liked what you said about Tammy. I thought it was cute…and they say there aren't any more good black men left."

"Yeah, there's some out here. That's for damn sure and you make sure that baby inside you knows that."

"I will."

"Good."

We were silent, watching the commercial for the next movie.

"You know we never really talked about how Rossi played us," Lauren reminded me.

"What's to say about the low-down dirty bastard?"

"I'm just sayin'…"

"Ain't no use crying—he played us," I told her.

"I'm never going to forget how he done us. Shit, I could be getting my life together by now."

"Maybe it wasn't in the cards, you know?"

"Well, I'm not the type to let someone get over on them."

"Yeah, but you ain't the one with Stallings breathing down your neck either. Don't you know that fool lost his job in narcotics over the stunt we pulled on the grand jury? He's pissed about it, too, 'cause he hates chasing killers."

Lauren crossed her arms saying, "Well, I want my money."

"Forget about it. Rossi is long gone by now."

18

On my way down to the garage, Lex came in and before she had a chance to shut the door, Lil'Man began to cry out for her in his playpen that was stuffed inside my kitchen next to the table. It had been days since he had seen his mother and Lauren wanted to know the reason why.

Lauren said, "So, how long you gonna keep this up?"

"Excuse me?" Lex questioned.

"What, you can't hear or something?"

"Yeah, I can hear, but you ain't saying nothing." Lex dropped to her knees, picked up Lil'Man and then began showering him with kisses and hugs.

"I'm talking about how long you're gonna keep this up, Lex. Coming and going and leaving your son here with me while you're out in the streets doing whateva..."

"Yeah, I'm doing whatever."

"You sure are."

"Well, whatever got me a job..." Lex sang.

"Say what?"

"You know that guy Robby?"

"You mean the trick that wouldn't leave you alone?" Lauren asked.

From what I heard from Lauren, this fool Robby had fallen for the loving Lex was putting on him, and all he ever wanted to do is lay up in her every chance he could get.

"Yup, the one and only. Well, that's where I've been staying and I guess it's just too good for that nigga—and he don't want nobody else looking at me at the club 'cause he said he was getting me an apartment in a few days. So you, Lil'Man and I are outta here. So, now you can have your place back, West," Lex, said. "We're moving out."

Lauren gave me a look and jumped in quick. "Hold on. I didn't say I was moving into no apartment with a nigga who is footing the bills."

"He ain't paying for shit. Well...maybe first month, whatever we work out," Lex clarified.

"So how the rent gonna get paid?" Lauren asked.

"Nigga is getting me a job at his advertising firm." Lex smiled and began to chant. "I'm gonna be workin'...I found me a job..."

Lauren put her hand on her hip. "Doing what?"

"Answering phones, making his contacts—shit, whatever he needs. Yup, he's giving me a job at his company."

"Look, I'm happy that you got a job. But I don't know, Lex?"

"Why not? I will go to work and you watch Lil'Man 'cause I know for a fact I ain't going to be able to pay rent, groceries and utilities plus childcare. You take care of him and we set 'cause I can handle the rest."

Lauren shot me a look, and then took a deep breath. "Look, Lex, I'm not going to be able to run after Lil'Man too much longer."

"Why not?"

"Because I'm about to have my own child."

"Lauren, what the hell you talking about?"

"Just what I said; I'm having a baby."

Lex didn't say another word. She walked over to Lauren and placed her hand on her stomach. "O...my damn. Girl, you...are pregnant!"

"You don't have to tell me. I already know," Lauren told her.

All of a sudden, Lex looked at me. "Damn, West, you don't waste any time, do you?"

"Hold up. Hold up. Unh, unh. I didn't have anything to do with it."

"West is not the father of this baby," Lauren told Lex, then grabbed her by the hand and pulled her into the kitchen.

I sat on the couch for a while watching the television until I got motivated enough to go out into the garage to do some more work. Lauren started to tell her sister about her child's father. I didn't want to hear anything about that nigga. I had heard enough. It really didn't sit too well with me that he wasn't returning any of Lauren's phone calls. I finished some work in the garage and when I came back in, they were still trying to figure out what they were going to do about leaving or not. I overheard Lauren tell Lex that she would just rather stay with me—that way she wouldn't be in debt to this nigga Robby. When Lauren asked me if she could stay with me, I told her sure—she was turning out to be a good friend.

19

Lex decided to take her son and move in with her trick. I spent the next few weeks trying to make ends meet while Lauren worked at the restaurant, if she felt up to it. I didn't know much about babies but I thought Lauren should have at least been to see a doctor being so close to four months along. Not having very much money to pay for the visit or insurance kept Lauren away. Then I had an idea. Mrs. Bullock thought her car wasn't spitting out enough air conditioning so I installed a brand-new one when I could've easily laced it with refrigerant. And on top of that, I charged her an extra twenty percent. I gave what I took from Mrs. Bullock to Lauren to go visit a doctor and decided to go with her.

"Thanks for coming with me, West."

"Not-a-problem," I told her—my eyes were all over the room.

"You're scared, aren't you?"

I was standing next to Lauren as she sat on a table while the female technician rubbed some type of jelly on her stomach. It was a first for me ever being in any type of hospital or doctor's quarters with a woman being worked on. Lauren's doctor requested an ultrasound. It didn't take long for the tech to begin circling Lauren's stomach with some computer doodad. She told us to look into the monitor that hung from the wall so we could see what was going on inside Lauren's stomach. I didn't know what the hell I was looking at. Everything seemed so fuzzy inside of Lauren and my first reaction was the baby was all fucked-up and shit; especially when the nurse didn't say much. She just kept talking to herself and pausing the freak'n screen for some reason. Then she began to show us parts of the baby. It was amazing and Lauren was damn near to tears—no doubt her hormones again.

The tech said, "You want to know the sex of the baby?"

"Yes!" Lauren shot back.

"Are you sure?" the tech asked again.

Lauren looked at me. "Should I find out, West?"

"Well, how you gonna find out if she don't tell you?"

"When it comes outta me, nigga…but I don't want to wait."

The tech shot me a look and laughed. "So you want to know?"

"Sure, tell me," Lauren told her.

The tech double-checked, then said for a third time, "You really want to know?"

I had to interrupt the bullshit. "She said yes, so would you go head already."

"It's a boy. Lauren, you're having a boy!"

On the way home Lauren was all smiles. Lauren told me if she ever was going to have a child, she wanted it to be a boy. I didn't realize how close she was to going down to the abortion clinic until Lauren became emotional again and told me she almost made a terrible mistake. Lauren really must have been hyped because she fixed me a nice meal when we returned—fried chicken, mashed potatoes, gravy and a nice salad with all the trimmings. Afterwards I had a couple of shots of E&J cognac and made my way to bed. About five minutes into my much-needed sleep, I heard my bedroom door open and kinda tightened up when Lauren pulled back the covers on the other side of the bed and slid in next to me.

"Thanks for doing that for me today."

I took a swig of my glass of ice water I had sitting on my nightstand and swished it around. "Ain't no problem, you needed it. The baby needed it."

Lauren snuggled up closer to me. "West, ain't no man ever did nothing like that for me before."

"What? Take you to the doctor?"

"No, show me some concern. I've been thinking about it all day."

"Like I say, there's plenty of good men around."

"And you're one of them." Lauren moved even closer until our bodies were touching. Then she kissed me. It was a short kiss but it awakened me in more ways than one. I didn't say anything; her kiss was good. It wasn't until her kiss that I thought about my final kiss with Tammy. Something about Lauren's lips was especially nice but I couldn't figure it the hell out. Then she kissed me again and I realized she had cold but very sensual lips and it turned me the hell on. Lauren's lips were perfect—dark, plump and very soft. She kissed me again. This time I kissed her back. Lauren looked at me, then smiled and her eyes went down to her pajama top. She began to unbutton it, then told me to take it off her. I enjoyed her aggressiveness; she knew exactly what she wanted and I didn't have to guess. When I finished, she kissed me again. This time longer—her lips had my head spinning like she was the first girl I'd ever kissed on a playground. I was amazed that I felt that way. I knew she must really be special to make a nigga's head spin. For the next couple of hours we did things that I never thought about doing with her—not because she wasn't attractive but because we had turned into friends and the things we did; they were all good.

➤ ➤ ➤

I came out my room the next morning and Lauren was sitting on the couch. I saw her hang up the phone when I walked in. Her arms were crossed but she smiled when she saw me standing there.

"Hey, sleepyhead."

"What's up?"

"Nothin' much."

I grabbed some juice and sat across from her. We just looked at each other. She blushed and I smiled.

"Tell me something."

"Anything."

"What we did last night? Does that make the baby mine since we did it?" She began to laugh at me. "Why you laugh'n? I'm serious. I ain't never did nothing like that before."

"You ain't knocked boots before, West?"

"Not with a pregnant woman."

"How you know?"

"What?"

"How you know you haven't done it before with a pregnant woman?"

I thought about her question. "Well, I don't know. But is it safe? Can we do that? I mean—now you got my DNA all up in you?"

Lauren's laugh was harder now. "West, shut the fuck up, nigga…it's okay."

"You sure?"

"Yes."

We sat still for a second.

"So, who was that on the phone?"

"You really want to know?"

"I asked, didn't I?"

"The baby's father."

"What'd he have to say?"

"Nothing."

"What do you mean, *nothing*?"

"Just what I said. Nigga said he ain't trying to have no kids. And told me good luck, then hung up."

When Lauren told me that shit, I made her give me his name and where I could get in touch with his punk ass. I didn't know what I was going to do or if I was going to do anything at all. At least I had his information just in case.

20

At first Stallings not being around made me kind of nervous because I didn't know what he was up to. Then all of a sudden, he started to bare his ugly ass face again. He called me down twice to the station and showed up once at my place. Even though he scared the shit out of me, acting like he had something on me when I knew he didn't, I couldn't trust his ugly ass. I wasn't trying to have Tammy's murder pinned on me just because he couldn't find anyone else to put it on. The police had been notorious for that type of shit in Atlanta when it comes to a black man. Plus, the word on the streets claimed judges were working with private industries to keep prisons full to capacity. But I wasn't going down on a prison roster. I would have left town if things had gotten any hotter for me; even though I was innocent.

After Tammy's murder, I tried to forget about it all—not think about it or imagine if she called out to me before she died. I really thought it was one of those freakish things that happen from time to time to people you know in life. Tammy wasn't the first person in my life who'd been found murdered. I had three friends who were killed before her. None of them were female though and I hadn't shared as much with them as I did Tammy. They were all killed over stupid shit.

My man Triggs was killed because of a drunk driver who was charged with murder. One of my closest friends, Jimmy, was killed right around the corner on my block because he cheated a young boy out of some weed when he went to cop for him. Then it was a longtime friend named Arthur whose wife smoked him after she found out he'd been stepping out with a twenty-two-year-old and knocked her up. So I had learned to put death as it really was—a part of life.

Those times that I really did think about Tammy's death were in a moment of drinking. That's when it became hard to deal with. Tammy didn't trust many people and whoever killed her she had to trust. The whole time we'd been seeing each other she had only been tight with a few of her girls, her family and that nigga Todd.

On a whim I decided to go see Todd—to find out what the hell he knew about Tammy's murder because it was really strange to me that the nigga never came over to say jack shit after she was gone.

I knew where Todd stayed because one night I made Tammy tell me after we had an argument about him. He had two places. One was twenty minutes or so away from me; the other out in Decatur close to Henry County on a dirt road. Tammy said he didn't go out there much, only when he wanted to walk in the woods or fish or something. I took my chances finding him at his place closest to me because I didn't have enough gas in Lauren's car for a drive out to Henry County.

I pulled up on the side of his house. It wasn't much. Looked like it was a ranch with three sides brick, but the yard needed some work. It was close to three in the afternoon so I wasn't sure if anyone was home or not. When I stepped on the porch I could barely hear a television. I knocked on the door and all of a sudden I couldn't hear the television set anymore. I knocked again, then again.

"Yeah…who is it?"

"West, I'm look'n for Todd."

There was a pause before the door opened. Todd looked past me into the street, then directly at me. "Yeah? What you want?"

"Came to talk."

"'Bout what?"

"Tammy."

"What 'bout her?"

"Negro, give the dead some respect."

Todd stepped back, widened the door, and then let me in. It was dark inside. All the curtains in the house were drawn. I followed him down a hallway. He didn't have furniture in his living or dining rooms, but when we stepped down into the sunken family room it was completely furnished and full of high-tech equipment. He had a high-tech chair sitting in front of one of those fly-ass, big-screen, high-definition television sets and nice black speakers everywhere. It was like double surround sound up in there. He sat in his chair and pointed toward another a few feet away from him.

"So what about Tammy?"

I sat down. "You know she dead, right?"

"Yeah, I heard that. Her sister told me. That's fucked-up."

Todd's voice was hard and I didn't appreciate it. I looked at him strong and asked him if he had a problem with me.

He moved a bit in his chair and said, "Naa...why you say that?" His eyes let me know he had an attitude.

Without delay I let him know if he had something to say—then maybe it was a good thing I did pay him a visit so he could get it off his chest.

He said, "A nigga just venting, that's all."

"You vent'n, hunh?"

"Yeah."

"'Bout what?"

"I hear poe-poe been questioning you about her death."

"You heard that?"

"That's right."

"From who?"

"The man himself, Captain Stallings."

"Stallings?"

"That's right, nigga."

"What the fuck he talk'n to you about me for?"

Todd shook his head, then looked down at the floor. "Don't know, Black. He came over here a few times. Ask me some shit about you and after all the questions he been asking, I thought he was thinking you the one who done killed Tammy."

I knew Stallings was trying to pin the shit on me. I toned down a bit because I needed some info from Todd now. I took a deep breath after I looked over his place again. "So, what kind of questions?"

"Why, nigga?"

"'Cause I wanna know. Fuck you, talk'n *why*?"

Todd wasn't helping me stay calm with his ignorant questions.

He had an eerie smile on his face. "You do the shit, Black? Did you kill her? 'Cause you know her family about to get up in your ass—and when they do, I'm going to watch every bit of it."

The way Todd was acting was the main reason I didn't even think about going to Tammy's funeral. It would have been just too much drama. I slowed and tried to gain my bearings.

"Nigga, I ain't kill anybody. Look, the night Tammy was killed she left me a note and said that she would be back but it never happened. That's all I know."

Todd began to shake his head. "Well, Stallings told me you might have killed her."

"Why would he say some shit like that?"

"He said it, after I told him Tammy told me that you got upset when I came over there; especially the time when I brought them groceries over the day before she died."

"I was mad, nigga!" I stood up, thinking I was about to blow. "But I wouldn't kill her over the shit. And why the fuck you spread'n hate to Stallings?"

"That ain't no hate; trust, those were facts," Todd said.

I wanted to reach out and pop Todd in the mouth but the thought of Stallings being over there talking about me was enough to make me keep my composure. Todd started fumbling around with his remote.

"What else you wanna know? I gotta get back to my shit," he said.

"Did you fuck Tammy?"

I don't know why I asked the question. It just came out. He was surprised as I was that I popped the question.

"Nigga, what?"

I inched closer to him. "You heard me. Did-you-fuck-her?"

Todd started to laugh like it was the best joke he'd ever heard. "Nigga, get out of here. I ain't gonna answer no stupid shit like that."

When I started to make my way to the front door I heard Todd's big screen pop back on. He was watching the movie *Training Day*. He noticed me when I turned to look at it.

He smiled and said, "Yo', this shit right here is tight. *Training Day*. Tammy told me you went to see this. How'd you like it?"

I looked at him, then at the movie again and walked out before I did kill the punk ass nigga.

21

Once again, Lauren saved the day and brought home a hot meal for my growling stomach. When I saw her bring it through the front door the differences between her and Tammy (God rest her soul) were like Hennessey and a half-pint of Mad Dog 20/20. Tammy complained about the food not being in the house. Lauren did something about it without disrespecting me.

Lauren walked in with a brown paper sack that was leaking a hell of an aroma even though it was covered up tight with aluminum foil. Lauren was spoiling me and I smiled as she put the chow on the table: peppered steak, brown rice, squash and hot rolls. As soon as it was all out of the bag, I had at it.

"I was the cook today at work, West. It's good, ain't it?"

"Sure the hell is. Who taught you to cook like this?"

"My mama did. She taught me a lot. Too bad we ain't speaking anymore."

"Why not?"

Lauren thought for a minute. "'Cause she didn't like how I was living my life. But it don't matter, just enjoy, okay."

"Good looking out…again. This is right on time."

"I like doing for you, West. As nice as you've been to a sister—who wouldn't?" Lauren sat down at the table and nibbled from a buttered roll.

"Do they know you bring'n this shit home damn near every night?"

"They know what they need to know."

"You go'n to eat?"

"Nope, I eat enough at work." Lauren poured some juice from the jug into my cup.

"Do me a favor, okay?"

"What is it?"

"Lean over and look on my forehead and see if I have *punk-sucker-ass nigga* written on it anywhere."

She smiled, then sang my name, "West...?"

"Go 'head, check."

"No—you don't have that shit on your forehead, nigga."

"Then why do I feel like I'm getting played?"

"You feel like that?"

"Hell yeah, sure do. Let's rewind the shit for a minute. Just a few months ago, that fuck'n judge knew I couldn't miss any days working my garage 'cause I needed to make money. I asked the man as nice as I could to give a nigga some leniency but the son of a bitch told me it was my duty to serve on the freaking jury and I should be proud."

"I remember. I was right there," Lauren reminded me.

"Then Rossi fucks me and sticks the shit all the way in without any kind of lubrication."

"It hurt me, too," Lauren confessed.

"And today, I went over to see Todd..."

"Todd?"

"That's right—Tammy's so-called *friend* that used to hang around here. When I asked him a few questions, he tried to get brand-new with me, then told me that he told Stallings some ill shit about me not liking him and getting mad when he hung out with Tammy."

"He said that?"

"Yeah, he said it. Then when I asked him if he fucked Tammy..."

Lauren interrupted, "Wait, you asked him that?"

"Hell yeah, sure did, but he didn't answer. He just laughed in my face until I thought I was going to have to beat him down."

"You shouldn't have asked him that, West."

"Why the fuck not?"

"'Cause that gave him something on you. Guys are a trip when it comes to that. They always want to have another man to think they've conquered what another has. It's a game."

"I don't give a damn. I wanted to know if she fucked over me, too."

Lauren put down her roll. "Why you worried about it, West? Forget about it; it's over between you two."

"Shit ain't that easy, Lauren. Some things I just need to know."

Lauren picked her roll back up, bit into it and slammed it down on the table. Her eyes were narrowed, her jaws tight as she chewed.

"What? You mad 'cause I asked?"

Lauren stood up saying, "No, I'm not mad. Don't mean anything to me. We're just friends anyway, right?" Then she walked away but asked me again, "Right?"

> > >

I finished my meal while Lauren sat on the phone talking to Lex. I gathered from their phone conversation that Lauren wasn't totally mad at me. She was pissed and bent all out of shape because that punk of hers who she slept with on a whim told her to forget about getting anything or any support for her child. Come to find out he told her if she tried to get any money from him for their baby he was going to leave the city. I don't know if Lauren was talking loud so that I could hear what was going on with her situation or what. But I know I didn't like what I was hearing. I thought about how he was treating her off and on for about forty-five minutes while I watched *Sports Center* in my room. I didn't appreciate his punk ass playing her.

I walked through the living room and heard Lauren tell Lex that she would watch Lil'Man for a few hours the next day. I finally went out to the garage since we'd just turned the clocks forward an hour. Thank God I had a little work to do. I had a tune-up and an oil change to do for paying customers. I finished them both. As I swept down my bay, Mrs. Bullock drove up and punched on her horn on the way in. It took her a little while to get out of the car.

"Hey, Mrs. Bullock, you doing all right?"

"I'm fine, West." She always smiled.

"What can I do for you? That air blow'n right, ain't it?"

"Oh, child, shit yeah. Sometimes it gets too cold for me. I just came by to see if you would keep her clean for me—you know on a regular basis. I was thinking about bringing her over once or twice a week for a wash. You think you can do that for me?"

"You know I can." I noticed Stallings drive past the shop. He rolled past me like he was searching for pussy or something, very slowly. I looked at him hard. Tried to tell him with my eyes that I had nothing to do with Tammy's killing. He gave me a look back like "you're a lying punk" and drove out of my sight.

"Everything all right, son?" Mrs. Bullock wanted to know.

"Fine, Mrs. Bullock. Everything's fine."

"Well, how much you charge me?"

I was thinking on my price. Mrs. Bullock had long money. She had retirement and pension money plus all the loot her husband left her. "For you Mrs. Bullock, forty dollars a pop. Keep her sparkling for you, too."

She thought for a second. "Okay, son, that sounds good. Forty is good. I just don't want to go to anybody to do my car. You know how it is. They try to up the price on me and play me roundabout," she said. "You know, I always say hell going to break loose if I find out somebody playing me roundabout and that's for sure."

For some reason I believed her, too. I always thought Mrs. Bullock carried heat with her, more than likely in the oversized purse she would always lug around that was probably full of medicines and pills and whatever a lady over seventy needed, but I wasn't sure. I did overhear an old man talking about her at a bar one night when the topic was city politics and some of the past leaders of Atlanta. He said in her younger days Mrs. Bullock would step to any chick who'd approached her husband and whoop her ass if need be. I told Mrs. Bullock that I didn't blame her one bit for standing strong for her shit and not being played. She let me know she would drop the car off later and I watched Mrs. Shirley Bullock as she got in her car and drove off.

When she was no longer in sight, I decided I was going to take her advice when it came to Stallings because if I didn't, I would get locked up soon. I just knew I would. The possibility of living in a cell was not what I had planned on doing. Stallings' drive-by past my place of business was just all too real. That crazy-looking bastard was not going to have the pleasure of tossing my ass in jail because he couldn't find anyone else. I decided right then and there, there would be no more playin' ol' West roundabout and that was for damn sure. I had to take care of business and somehow get Stallings off my back.

22

It was close to ten at night. I was in the bed with one eye open watching television. Lauren peeked into my room and let me know she was on her way out to fill up her gas tank, then to the store for milk and shortbread cookies to satisfy her craving. I didn't want Lauren out in the streets so late so I decided to go for her.

The car stopped when I was halfway to the gas station. I thought it was my payback for charging Mrs. Bullock so much to wash her car—that freaky karma thing everybody talks about. Riding in Lauren's car was a crapshoot anyway. The gas gauge was dead as hell, even if the tank was full of gas. It took me fifteen minutes to walk to the gas station. Thirty minutes to talk the damn Arab into letting me hold a gas can; ten dollars to use it with an eight-dollar deposit, then another twenty-five minutes or so to lug the shit back to where I broke down. Finally, I was behind the car facing the street waiting for the gas to funnel through and I couldn't believe my luck because that's when I saw the sparkling grille of my Caddy zoom right past me.

➤ ➤ ➤

I dropped the can, hopped behind the wheel of the car, started it up and did a U-turn to follow the son of a bitch who was behind the wheel of my car. I passed three cars before I saw my Caddy again. Whoever stole my car didn't even change the license plate and was driving my baby with the courtesy light on above the passenger's side draining my battery. I couldn't see who the hell was in it. That's why I always liked my diamond in the back—complete privacy. We drove about ten minutes before the car turned into a neighborhood and that's where I ran out of gas again. I took Lauren's pistol out of the dash. There was no other choice; I had to jump out and give chase. I tired quickly, barely making it one block and soon I found myself bent over at the knees trying to catch my breath. I could barely get enough air up in my lungs. When I finally looked up again, all I could see was the back of my car fade into the night.

I wasn't giving up. I started to walk. I didn't know where I was and didn't care. I wanted my car back. I promised myself I wouldn't be played round-about again and I meant that. After a while it got to a point where I had to just start going down streets in the neighborhood to look for my car. And I was getting confused while doing it because all of the houses in the neighborhood looked alike. I had to be cautious walking around and how I looked into the driveways with cars because all I needed was the police to pull up on my black ass, find the pistol on me—then take me back downtown.

I looked for my car at least an hour and it had to be close to midnight when I sat down to rest on a street curb. When I got back on my feet I looked down the street and sitting up under a streetlight was my sweet-heart. I walked up to my baby and inspected the outside. She was still intact. If I would have had my keys I would have jumped in and taken off. But I didn't, so I opened the back door on the passenger side because I knew the lock was broken. I then sat my tired ass in the back seat. I didn't know what I was going to do once whoever was driving the car came out, but I knew my car was going home with me.

➤ ➤ ➤

The clock on my dashboard read two-fifteen. By now Lauren must have been worried. A regular run to the store and to fill up was a fifteen-minute trip, twenty max. I was seconds away from dozing off; the chase on foot was about to take its toll. I hadn't run like that in at least twenty years. All of a sudden I heard footsteps inching closer to the car and all I could do was crouch down in the back seat and wait for the bastard to put the key in the ignition and start to drive off.

Perfume hit me through the car before the door was even opened. A female stole my shit? A lady? Hell no. Her fragrance smelled good though and I was relieved that it was only one person, female at that, to handle to get my car back. I thought she must be one of those roguish bitches though to steal a car, so I was prepared to kick her ass like I would a man if need be. Then my mind wondered, *what kind of woman who smelled so good would even think about jackin' cars?*

After she sat behind the wheel, she didn't start the car as quickly as most would at two in the morning. She began to fumble through her purse, then took out a small bottle of mouthwash, threw back a hell of a portion and began to swish it around. She was using that strong shit, *Listerine*. The timing seemed perfect. I arose from the back seat and placed my pistol hard to the side of her head.

"Swallow," I told her.

Her eyes bugged out. She shook her head no and reached for the door.

I grabbed her arm. "Bitch-I-said-swallow."

She rolled her eyes at me without turning her head completely to see me, still holding the burning concoction in her mouth. While I watched her struggle, I moved back so she wouldn't spit the liquid in my face and burn my eyes.

"Last chance," I told her as mean as I could sound.

She did.

And I watched her gag for a few seconds as it went down her pie hole and settled in her stomach.

"Now, is this your car?"

She nodded yes while she struggled with the aftertaste.

"Since when?" I asked over her hacking.

She looked at me like she didn't understand. From what I could see through the darkness, mama was fine. She was a white girl who was tanned, bronze like a Rican or some shit. She was slim, and had a tight shirt that exposed some gigantic tits.

"How'd you get this car, lady?"

She spoke slowly and very clearly, "Are-you-going-to-kill-me?"

"I don't know yet," I told her. Then I pushed the pistol again on her head. "Where'd you get it?"

"A friend."

"Name?"

"Rossi."

She told me her name was Rita and after I verified the nigga Rossi was one in the same that played me for my grand jury earnings, out of spite, I gripped my pistol extra tight. I could tell Rita knew I was heated. I thought about taking over at the wheel. But I knew she was scared to die. So I made her drive: that way I didn't have to worry about her hurting herself or me. She asked me if I was going to kill her at least six times. She didn't know it at the time, but it was Rossi who I wanted.

"What you got so much to live for?" I asked her. Maybe Rossi gave her some of my money or something so I began to go through her purse to see how much she was carrying. I only found two tens. Then she told me she had four hundred in her shirt and told me to take it and leave her alone.

"Give it to me," I told her.

She did quickly.

"Now answer my question."

"What?"

"What you got so much to live for? You hiding something with punk ass Rossi?"

"I just like living," she said back. "I need to get home."

"That makes two of us," I told her. "Where you live?"

"Downtown," she said. "In a loft."

"Roommate?"

"No, it's my place."

"Let's go there. Did Rossi tell you whose car this was?"

She looked at me. "No. Is it yours?"

"You're damn right."

"I didn't know."

Somehow I believed her. I didn't like how she looked at me though. She was tuned into me like I was one of those mothafuckas on *America's Most Wanted* or something. I took the pistol from my lap and placed it under the seat as she drove.

"You ain't got to look at me like that no more, okay. I ain't a crazy nigga. I just don't like being played."

"So, Rossi played you, too?" Rita wanted to know.

"What do you mean, *too*?"

"He owes me money," she said. "That rat bastard."

"Yeah, you're right. That makes two of us."

"Not surprising, he owes everybody."

I said, "What he owe you for?"

She looked over at me as she made a right-hand turn. "Sex."

I reached inside my jacket and pulled out a cigarette. "So, you're in the business, hunh?"

"Yeah and I wish you hadn't made me swallow back there."

23

When we arrived at Rita's, I wasn't surprised that she didn't seem scared of me anymore. More than likely her experience with her tricks gave her the strength to put up with me. I watched her though once we got inside her place. If she was a ho, she had a piece somewhere. I was sure of it. When she walked into her bedroom, I went with her. When she went to the kitchen to make drinks, I was right beside her. I didn't want her to turn the situation around on me. As far as I was concerned, every ho owned a pistol or at least should.

Rita gave me her cordless and I called Lauren. Lauren couldn't believe my luck. I was glad that she didn't ask me about her car. I was sure the police had already towed it or placed a few tickets on it. Lauren told me to do whatever I had to do to find Rossi. She didn't have to worry about that because that was my plan.

I sat on Rita's couch and she brought over a drink as I looked over her loft. It was nice. She had expensive art and a very professional contemporary paint job on the walls. Her furniture was comfortable enough to lie down on and fall into a deep sleep. Her place looked like a professional ho lived in it, ready at all times. We sat on the couch for a few minutes before she finally spoke.

"So, I guess you want me to take you to Rossi?"

"Damn right. Ain't no guessing behind that shit."

"What's in it for me?"

"Look, you're not in the position to bargain."

"Bullshit...If you were going to hurt me, you woulda by now," she said. "I know that much."

I decided then that Rita could hold her own. "You know where he is?"

"Sure do."

"Tell me?"

"How much?"

She was about to piss me off. "I don't have a dime to give."

"How much does he owe you?" Rita wanted to know.

"Thousands," I told her.

Her eyes kind of widened. "Thousands, or hundreds of thousands?"

"Thousands," I repeated. She didn't need to know but her eyes didn't believe me.

"I'm going to need five thousand for the info," she decided. "And my four hundred back—I sucked a real little nasty dick and fucked a butt ugly man for that money. Trust me, it wasn't pretty."

I stared at her and tried to get some perspective of Rita when I reached into my pocket to give her back her money. Shit, she was just like me, a spineless opportunistic soul looking for a dollar to line her pockets.

"Fuck it, done." Rita held out her hand and I gave her back her bills. I told her I would give her the five grand but she didn't know it was coming out of Rossi's end as soon as we caught up with him.

Rita gripped her money with her fist and crumbled it up. "I have his telephone number, too," Rita let me know. "It's in my bedroom."

"Do I need to follow you?"

"Not unless you have other business you want to discuss."

"Always on duty, hunh?"

"It's all about the money, baby. And it's money I need."

When I told her I was broke, I meant that shit. "I don't think so."

"By the way, what's your name?"

"West...my name is West."

Rita stood up from the couch, then walked over to the television set. Our conversation seemed to loosen her up even more. She popped in a tape in the recorder, then walked back into her room. Rita's walk was long and seductive. When the tape started I was forced to keep an eye out for Rita and the other peeled on the screen. The tape was a porno of Rita. She was riding a big black guy who looked like he was all the way up in her and enjoying what he was doing. I'd watched porno before but not one so hot and real. Rita rode her partner, then she would stop, take a taste of his licorice stick, plop it back in her wetness and then was back off to the races. Suddenly the tape stopped. Rita was standing on the wall just outside the hallway that led to her bedroom with the remote in her hand.

"Surprised? It's something I do for fun. Sometimes I show it when a guy comes over if he can't get it up."

"Shit's better than Viagra, hunh?"

"There's nothing else like it." She walked toward the couch. "Have you ever been on tape?"

"Not my thing."

"I was thinking about going to L.A. and making a career in the business. What do you think? Would I be a star?"

➤ ➤ ➤

Rita gave me Rossi's telephone number and his address. The number she gave me was completely different from the digits I got from Rossi. Rita said Rossi had moved into a new place a few days earlier but he was not home. He went out of town and would be back in the morning.

I was not going to take the chance of leaving her until I found Rossi so I kept Rita close to me. We sat on the couch and for some reason Rita wanted to watch her performance on tape and give me blow by blow of the action while we sipped on drinks. It was like *Sports Center* up in that bitch. Rita analyzed every position she and the big black stud took on— every pump, every hump and every lick in-between. Rita was proud of how she served it up. Come to find out, Rita had numerous tapes, and a couple of hours and quite a few adjustments for me later, she wanted to know if I liked her work.

"Yeah, yeah, it's good. I'm impressed." I really was; Rita was kinky, verbal and versatile.

She said, "But…?"

"But what?"

"You were going to say something else? C'mon, go 'head and say it."

"Not judging you but you don't even know that nigga. He could be burn'n or something."

"Money makes you do shit you never dreamed of, West," Rita said. Then she put her hand in my lap. "Besides, I get checked at the doctor's on a regular basis; even a ho likes to stay healthy."

I looked down at her hand. "Tell me about it. Money will fuck your head up."

Rita moved her hand toward my meat; she knew damn well I was hard as a rock. "You ever paid for it?"

I removed Rita's hand when I felt her getting closer. "No. But I've paid for what I've done, plenty."

She said, "Well, since we're waiting on the sun to rise, I wouldn't mind exploring a bit with you; we'll just make it a part of the five grand you're giving me. Plus, I'm so horny." Rita stood up and put in yet another tape of her X-rated erotica and pushed play. She sat back down, this time on my lap and began to nibble on my ears as though she knew it was my spot. I couldn't help but go from her on the screen to all up in my grill, close and personal. I was getting weak. Her fingers stroking my face made a brother want to do better than her Mandingo warrior handling her on the tape. Rita stood up, then reached down to pull her dress over her head. When her dress got to her mountains she hesitated.

"Get ready, 'cause when Rita wants to do it, it's the best," she said.

When her dress came off, her nipples began to speak to me. I stood up and my intentions were to put them in my mouth, suffocate my face in her bosom. My tongue reached for her right nipple and I grazed it as she pulled back teasing, and the sound of her moan made me want to throw her on the couch and take care of business, but I stopped right before I gathered both of her cantaloupes together to taste.

She looked at me. "What's wrong? You don't want to taste Rita?"

"I want to fill you up like you wouldn't believe, but I can't."

Rita looked at me disappointed but understanding. "Someone else?" She tried to reach down and touch what had been poking her in-between her legs through my pants.

I stepped back. "Maybe, yeah maybe it is."

24

I managed to get a few hours of sleep with one eye open with Rita laying her head on my chest. It was time to go see Rossi and I downed three cups of coffee before we left. In between the coffee and Rita going back and forth into her bedroom getting dressed, I found out as much as I could about Rita and how she ever got involved with Rossi in the first place.

Rita was from Minneapolis and couldn't wait until she was eighteen to break away from her overprotective parents to go to school in all places Seattle, Washington. She said she didn't last a year there because she fell in love with a guy from Portland. She followed him back to his hometown after he decided Seattle wasn't for him and she spent years trying to convince him she was the best thing that ever happened to him; even after he left her to marry someone else. Rita said after that long episode in her life she just felt like giving everything she was saving to anyone who would pay for it, and it turned out to become her full-time job that she wasn't ashamed of.

➤ ➤ ➤

It felt good to be behind the wheel of my car again. It needed washing and the alignment was too far to the right, but my baby was running smooth. Rita took me into Hapeville where Rossi was staying in a new apartment complex. That's when I remembered he told the jury he grew up there. I parked my car a block away inside the bay of a rundown car wash because I didn't know if the police were still watching Rossi or what I was really getting myself into. Plus, if I had to bust a cap in his ass I didn't want anyone to get my license plate on the getaway. Rita was nervous. She told me Rossi told her to never bring a soul to his place. Fuck that; we were on our way. I had Rita knock on the door.

"Yeah, who is it?" came from the other side. It was Rossi's voice for sure.

"It's me, Rita."

"Hold on a second."

I heard Rossi walk away from the door and I adjusted my pistol. I moved it from the small of my back to the front of my waistband. I wanted to get to it quick if his monkey ass was thinking about turning into Billy *BAD ASS*. Rita looked over at me as I stood on the side of the door. She was nervous but she wanted her money, too. Rita told me on the way over that Rossi made her feel like shit when he told her he didn't have her cash and didn't know when he would get it after he had run a tab going in and out between her legs for an entire weekend.

Rita didn't say, but I think it was a bit more personal between those two. She knew way too much of his business. In my book no man tells a woman so much if he didn't care for her just a little. Rossi began to fumble at the door, and then it was opened. Rita took about two steps inside and when Rossi turned his back to see her in, it was my opportunity and I bum-rushed the door.

Surprised, Rossi turned around and before he could say one word, I sucker-punched him in the jaw. He fell backwards into a mirror hanging on the wall, shattering the glass onto the floor. He held his jaw while on one knee and shook off the surprise. Then, with lightning speed, he began to charge at me over Rita's loud scream.

Rossi put his head down like a raging bull and rammed into me, pushing me back into a wall. He swung and I blocked his punch. I swung back and missed because he ducked. His next punch to my face connected drawing blood but the one I threw back, I'm sure came close to breaking his freaking nose. Just like a white boy, Rossi tried to get close to me and wrestle me down to the ground. I tried like hell not to allow him because I knew he was in shape and would probably crush my black ass. I kept him at a distance and felt myself tiring too quickly. Rossi didn't look like he was anywhere near tired. It was though he was just getting started, so I pulled my pistol and I be damned if he didn't pull his at the same time from the small of his back. At the same time, we both wanted to know, "Where's my money?!"

I was exhausted.

"Don't fuck with me, Rossi. Give me my money, man, or I'm going to cap your ass."

Rossi was pointing his pistol right back at me.

"What the fuck are you talking about?"

"My two-hundred grand—one for me, the other for Lauren."

"You got a lot of balls, man, coming back in here talking that shit after what you pulled."

I flinched my gun. "Punk, what're you talking about?"

He flinched back. "You stole the money, bitch. Don't think I don't know the fool who came over and took two-eighty from me wasn't working with you. Then had the nerve to leave me with twenty. What the fuck am I going to do with twenty grand?"

"How 'bout giving me what you owe me?" Rita interrupted.

I was still trying to catch my breath by leaning back against a wall but keeping my pistol aimed at Rossi. "What are you talking about? What guy?"

Rossi said, "Todd. I'm talking about Todd."

When I heard his words I slid down against the wall and dropped my pistol to the floor.

25

Rita fixed us drinks and gave us both cold compresses for our aches. I was sprawled out lying back on Rossi's couch, exhausted. He kept asking Rita if his nose was broken. I told him it wasn't because if it was, he couldn't stand it. My lip was cut, but I didn't worry about it. I wanted to find out about the money and Todd. After about three drinks we were well-rested and ready to talk.

"So tell me what the fuck happened?" I asked after Rossi made sure I had nothing to do with him losing my and Lauren's money and a huge portion of his.

He sat up and pushed on his nose a couple of times before he spoke. "It's like this. After I hung up the phone talking to you to meet at the club, three punk ass bastards busted in my place."

"And you say one of 'em was named Todd?"

"That's right. He was the leader. Some light-skinned cock sucker who said you and he was boys and working together."

"He said that?"

"That's what he said."

"Then what happened?"

"They beat my ass, then sat me in my own recliner and made me watch a tape."

Rita looked at Rossi. "A tape?"

"Yeah, definitely some sick shit, too."

"How so?" I wanted to know.

"It was Todd with a woman. I knew it was him because the camera was all in his face."

"So, what she look like?"

Rossi explained, "I couldn't tell you. They were careful not to show her face. Fucking camera work was like a damn movie or some shit. Most of the shit was shown from a distance. Anyway, I guess he'd just finished doing her or something because they were butt ass naked in the bed, giggling."

"So?"

"So, he mounted her again. I mean he was enjoying that pussy, man. Don't act like you don't know how the pussy feels the second time around? But after he was going for a couple of minutes, this sucker got real violent with her."

"Violent?"

"Yeah, started to slap her around and shit, then he snatched a pillowcase off the pillow and put it over her head."

"So? Sometimes it works for me," Rita said.

"Yeah, at first I thought they were joking around, getting a little kinky. But all of a sudden, the cameraman comes out the closet and when she hears the cameraman's voice she becomes hysterical and shit. Then this asshole Todd gets upset and starts to slap her around."

"For what?"

"Didn't say at first. But he started to finger her really hard until she told him to stop. Then this bastard had the nerve to tell the camera operator to zoom in close and I be damned if he didn't try to stick a beer bottle as far as he could inside her. Then he started saying shit like, '*How can I trust you now? Bitch, if you played him, ain't no telling what the fuck you'd do to me.*' Then he told her he didn't have any use for her anymore but thanked her for leading him to the pot of gold." Rossi stopped for a second and took a drink from his glass. "Then he started to beat her—I mean some brutal blows—and told whomever was handling the camera to zoom in again and then it was over."

"Dead?" I asked.

"Yup. He strangled her. I mean straight up and raw, took her breath right out of her. Then this crazed fool tells me he and his boys are going to do me if I don't give him all the money I had. Hey, I like breathing and gave him my money. He takes all of it, then throws twenty thousand back in my face and the keys to a shitty Caddy that he parked in my driveway and said that you wanted me to have it."

I sat and put everything going on together. "I think that punk killed my girl."

"Could be," Rossi said.

"And the Caddy is not shitty. It's one of a kind."

We drank damn near all the liquor Rossi had up in his place. Everyone was drunk and for a moment we tried to put everything that had happened in perspective while the liquor was doing its thing inside all of us. Rossi was flying high and Rita was not far behind as their raging hormones for one another were about to set the place on fire. The liquor had turned them both on and for the time being their tongues were lost in each other's mouths.

The liquor was having a different effect on me though. All I could think about was Tammy and the possibilities of Todd being her killer. I always knew that bastard was a little off upstairs, even more dangerous than he led Tammy to believe. It made me think I should have beat his ass when he brought the groceries over and tried to show me up in front of Tammy.

At first, it was kind of hard for me to digest what Rossi was slinging around about Todd—sticking him up for our loot. But there was no fucking way he could have made the story up so fast under the pressure of our fight. I made a vow that if Todd killed Tammy I would make things right. If what Rossi said was true about her being in the bed with Todd, it goes without saying Tammy played me foul by getting Todd's punk ass involved with my business dealings. But then again maybe he forced my business out of her, even though she didn't know much anyway. One thing

I knew for sure; I was going to find out what happened because the path led to Todd killing Tammy, taking our money and stealing my car.

> > >

I was right. Rossi and Rita were more than business associates. When I saw how they were going at each other in their drunken stupor, for a brief second I thought I should have done her myself. I don't know why my mind went in that direction, but I thought about what Lauren told me about men holding on to conquest. I wasn't any better than Todd in that sense because now Rossi was the one with the prize.

Rossi and Rita were drunk and lying on the floor together giggling and gaggling about every damn thing the other said. I had a feeling Rossi was satisfied with his twenty grand that Todd left him with and the freak show he was about to get from Rita; at least his ass wasn't in jail. The liquor had me paralyzed but I knew what was going on right before my eyes, especially when Rita took out one of her monstrous tits and fed it to Rossi.

I came close to putting the exact nipple in my mouth at her place. I took a long investigating look at Rita and decided there was no way her tits were real. *Just no way*. I'd never seen tits that perfect in my life. When they were in my face the night before, they were so tempting that it didn't cross my mind if they were real or not. Rossi was so drunk he couldn't even keep her in his mouth so he began to flick his tongue across her nipple fast as lightning. It drove Rita crazy and the sounds of pleasure that came out of her excited Rossi, even gave me a charge.

Rita tried to give Rossi her other tit by pushing it all up in his face. He tried to handle it but was too drunk. Rita laughed, and then stood up. She said something about how nice his tongue was moving and like the pro she was, Rita ripped off her dress and threw it at my feet across the room while I sat idle on the couch with my glass of Hennessey.

Rita was bold. There was no hesitation about her. I watched her walk over to Rossi as he sat on his knees, grab the back of his head, and straddle his face as his tongue disappeared. The scene was hot, even better than the movies Rita shared with me. The Rita I saw on screen was now live in action and didn't give a care in the world who was watching. I forced more liquor down and kept my eye on Rita as she used her partner's tongue. She was serious. She wanted to release and didn't give a damn who knew about it. I didn't want to seem like I was getting off on their shit so I grabbed Rossi's remote, turned on the television and began flicking through the channels. When I got to MTV there was some chick rapping to a pretty nice beat, chanting *"lick my neck, my back, my clit, just like dat."*

"Oh, my damn," Rita said. "That's my song. Do it, Rossi, lick it. That's right, get on beat."

I had no other alternative than to do the man thing and egg Rossi on. The night had become a freak show. Rossi was now underneath her and smacking like he was eating Thanksgiving dinner.

Rita looked over at me. "You want some of this, West?" She pushed Rossi's head upward and held it tight.

I didn't comment and laughed Rita off.

Rossi broke free, growling as though he was enjoying his last meal, and said, "Trust me, brother, it's enough for two."

"Shut up and eat me," Rita demanded. "C'mon, West, baby, what do you say?"

"I'll pass."

Rita flicked her tongue at me, then took Rossi by the hand and went toward the bedroom.

Rita looked back at me. "West, if you change your mind, don't bother to knock." Then she turned her hips in my direction and smacked her tight ass.

Rossi could barely stand and he looked over at me and held out his hand.

"Hey, West, gimme a condom, man." Rita turned and looked at him. "You got any condoms, West?" Rossi stumbled and Rita tried her best to hold him up.

I just shook my head at Rossi's stupid ass and told him, "Nigga, if she has anything—you already ate it."

Rita said, "Ain't that the truth—now get your drunk ass in here."

➤ ➤ ➤

While Rossi and Rita were getting their sex on, I called Lauren. I found the phone in the kitchen. Rossi was a neat freak. Everything in the kitchen was in place and washed up and put away, like he was expecting his mother or something. I sat at his table and dialed Lauren. The phone rang about five times before she answered, carefully and slowly.

"Hello."

"Lauren?"

"West?"

Lauren sounded scared to death about something. "Yeah it's me, what's wrong?"

"West, where have you been? I need you right away."

The panic in her voice brought my high down at least fifty percent.

"What's the matter?"

"I can't say over the phone. West, you need to come home."

Then the phone went dead. I stood for a moment to gather my thoughts, then took a few steps toward the bedroom where Rossi and Rita were. The door wasn't shut all the way and I peeked in and they were having at it— Rita getting it as hard as Rossi could give it to her doggy-style. I went back into the kitchen and noticed Rossi's keys on the countertop and placed them in my pocket. That way I knew he wouldn't be going anywhere until I got back. We had unfinished business to attend to. Plus the twenty grand Todd left him, by the rules of the street, was partly mine.

26

It was a fifteen-minute ride back to my place. When I got inside, Lauren and Lex were both on the couch. Lex had her head on her sister's shoulder and when they looked up at me, I could tell they'd been crying all night. They didn't want to answer me when I repeatedly asked what was wrong.

"It's Lil'Man. Lil'Man is dead," Lauren said.

Lex broke from the couch and ran into my bathroom, then slammed the door shut. I sat down next to Lauren.

"Dead? What the hell happened?"

"West, you have to do something," Lauren said in a panic.

"Lauren, I can't do anything if I don't know what's going on."

"Earlier today, Lex had to work. She called me and asked me to watch Lil'Man but I couldn't because I was feeling really tired. So, Lex took Lil'Man to work with her and that punk ass nigga who got her the apartment told her that she couldn't bring no kids inside his place of business and told her to get him out."

Lauren could tell I was confused and she tried to clear it up.

"So now, Lex has a dilemma. Her nigga tells her that if she doesn't hurry back to work he was going to fire her, plus not keep his promise of paying for the first three months' rent on her place."

"But what happened to Lil'Man? That's what I want to know."

"Lex didn't know what to do, so since she had my car, she sat him in the car by himself on the top ramp of the parking lot."

"It must have been ninety degrees today."

"West, I know…But Lex swears she kept going back and forth like every twenty minutes or so to check on him," Lauren tried to explain. "But then her punk ass nigga told her not to leave the front desk again or she was gone. So she said she left Lil'Man in the car for exactly one hour and when she got back to the car at lunchtime, he was gone."

I stood up from the couch and ran my fingers over the top of my head. This shit was serious. "Lauren, you can't leave no fuck'n baby in a car like that!"

"I know, West. Lex is going crazy—she loved that boy."

"So what did the police say?"

"Police?"

"Yeah, the police. Ya'll called the police, right?"

Lauren started to cry. "No—he's still out in the car, in your garage."

Just like Lauren said, Lil'Man was in the back seat of her car out in my garage. His body was face down and his Power Ranger blanket covered him up to his shoulders. The sight of his small body without any movement at all put me to tears. I hadn't prayed in a long time but I managed to say a few words for the little boy.

The sight of Lil'Man instantly took my high away and put fear and pain on me like I'd never known. This pain was definitely sharper than what I felt when my car was stolen, even cut deeper than when I really realized Tammy was gone; because the boy was so young and never had a fighting chance. I felt beads of sweat form on my forehead and so much anxiety that I wanted to just walk out of my garage and never turn back. This was trouble—a very big mess. When I opened the car door to remove Lil'Man, it was another world—full of darkness. It didn't help my nerves any when Lauren touched my arm right before I touched the baby.

She whispered, "So what you gonna do, West?"

"Look, don't-you-ever sneak up on me like that, okay?"

"Okay, okay—who else would be in here?"

"Shit, I dunno, Stallings—the Grim Reaper—just don't do that shit, understand." I tried to touch the small boy a few times but I just couldn't do it.

"By the way, he called," Lauren said. "He left a message for you to call him."

"Who called?"

"Stallings."

"Fuck-me." Lauren's information lit a fire under my ass. "Look, I have to do something about this—with the quickness."

Lauren said, "What?"

"I don't know—I mean the baby's dead. He's dead in my garage. Who else knows about this?"

"Just me, you, and Lex."

"Damn, I wish ya'll woulda called the police, Lauren. Why'd you bring him here?"

"Because you know the police, West. They would put her ass in jail and throw away the key. When a baby dies, they don't want to hear shit."

"I know, I know."

"Plus, Lex was scared, and she didn't know what to do. She didn't mean for this to happen—you know she didn't, West. She was just trying to make a living for the child and got caught up."

I really didn't know what to do. I had never been at a point in my life where I had no idea what to do in a situation. "Look, he's going to have to stay here until later. You go in and try to calm Lex down, okay? You know there's no way she's gonna be able to stay here after this, right?"

"I know."

"I got enough shit to worry about around here."

"So where will she go, West?"

"Uh, tell her, she has to go back to North Carolina or something."

"Go back home without the baby?"

"Look, you two figure that shit out, okay? All I know is she can't stay here."

"So what you gonna do?"

"I don't know. But I need some help, that's for sure."

➤ ➤ ➤

I locked up the garage extra tight, and then high-tailed it back over to Rossi's. I used my key to get in and I be damned if Rita and Rossi weren't still in the bed sleeping off their drunk. First things first; I had to return Stallings' call. I didn't want him to go over to my place and see Lil'Man dead in my garage. I had called Stallings so many times that I knew his number by heart. When he realized it was me on the other end of the phone, I could tell he thought he had me by the balls.

He said, "Where are you?"

"Why?"

"Because I need to talk to you, West."

"Talk to me? What the hell for? I told you everything I know."

"No, I think you've told me everything you want me to know," he said.

"Stallings, what are you talking about?"

"I have a witness."

"A witness? C'mon man, is that shit supposed to make me piss my pants or something?"

"If I were you, I would. Prison doesn't fit you."

"Bullshit. You're trying to frame me, Stallings."

"Listen jerk-off, I'm not asking you—we need to talk."

I wasn't going to prison for this shit. Hell no. Poe-poe wasn't framing me for Tammy's murder. I was beginning to feel the pressure though. "Look, I know who did it," I told Stallings. I wasn't one hundred percent sure but at least I had a hunch and it would buy me some time, I had hoped.

"Say what?"

"I said, I know who did it, but I need some time, to sort things out. Look, meet me tomorrow night," I told Stallings.

"Where?"

"Nikki's downtown. Ten o'clock."

After I finished with Stallings, a car horn began blasting away outside

Rossi's apartment. I went to the window and took a look behind the shades. It was a cab. Seconds later, Rossi and Rita came out the room. Rossi looked sluggish and fucked out and over. Rita kissed him on the cheek, and then gave me one, too. It had to be near seven in the morning.

"West, hun, that's my cab. I gotta run."

"Look, I'm sorry 'bout that mouthwash thing the other night. That shit must've burned to no end."

Rita playfully hit me on the arm. "You're right, it did—but don't worry about it. Listen, Rossi took care of me. He owes me no longer," she said.

"Good."

"If you guys need anything, you know where to find me."

Rita gave Rossi one last tongue-twisting kiss and she was out the door.

➤ ➤ ➤

Rossi put a wide grin on his face and looked around. "Whew…Man, can she go. Maybe you should've gotten a piece of that ass, too. Believe me, there's enough for two."

"Can't even think about pussy right now—and ain't she your woman?"

"At the moment she's an acquaintance, but she could be my woman."

"And you would let me fuck 'er?"

"I like to have shit on my girls. Dirty shit that I can always throw back in their faces when they start fucking up—because they always fuck up West, always." He began to laugh. Rossi lit his cigarette, then handed me his pack. "What's on your mind?"

"I gotta load of shit on my mind and you have to help me."

"Help you do what?"

"For one, we have to get our money back from the nigga who stole it. Plus, I need you to help me get out of hot water with Stallings because he thinks I killed Tammy. And I will tell you the rest when we get over to my place."

Rossi's voice raised an octave. "Punk ass Stallings? Working homicide?"

"Yeah…they moved him after we fucked him on your grand jury case and he's pissed about it, too, so you gotta help me."

"Say what?"

"That's right. We gotta do something to get him off my ass so we can get this money, nigga."

Rossi said, "Look man, I just got my ass out of hot water. I'm thinking about chalking this shit up as a fucked-up experience."

"The hell you are. I want my money. Nigga, don't be a bitch."

"No can do. I ain't getting involved in this shit. You fucking around with murderers now."

"Look, Rossi, if that's how you're going to play me, I'm going to Stallings and tell him why he lost his job in the first place. That alone—will probably get him his job back in narcotics. And then we both are going the fuck behind the steel because I won't do time alone. You know he wants you anyways; he told me himself." Stallings hadn't mentioned Rossi, but I had a feeling Rossi didn't want to deal with him anymore. He came entirely too close to going to jail.

"He said that?"

"That's what he told me," I lied.

"Okay, okay. Fuck that, I ain't going to prison, man. I can't do it."

"That's what I thought."

"So what else you need help with?"

"Get dressed and let's go to my place. I'll tell you when we get there."

27

I waited for Rossi to shower and then we took off in my car. On the drive over to my house I had to endure Rossi bitching about how I didn't give him enough time to put on something nice. His pretty boy bullshit not only got to me when he was facing trial but really was a bitch to deal with up close and personal. I told him it was probably better anyway that he didn't have his best on, especially after he found out what I needed his help with.

When we pulled up to my garage, I had Rossi get out and open the garage so I could pull in. Rossi was impressed with my setup. He couldn't believe I had it in me to run my own business. I didn't know what he meant by it. I told him that I had skills, and my recent drama was in no way an indication of how I'd been living before I sat down and had to listen to his case on jury duty. After I locked the garage again, Rossi wanted to know what was going on.

"Look, man, I need your help," I told him.

"I already told you I would help with Stallings," he said.

"Not Stallings, this is much bigger."

"Bigger than Stallings?"

"Much." I pointed toward Lauren's car and Rossi followed me over to it. "Look, before you go berserk, let me tell you I didn't have anything to do with this."

"What are you talking about?"

I opened the backseat of the car and pointed at Lil'Man. I didn't have to explain that he was dead.

Rossi took one look, then turned away and began walking toward the front of my garage. "Oh, hell no—I'm out of here."

"Hold up, Rossi. Shit, wait a minute."

"No...way. I'm telling you...no...no...no."

"Look, Lauren's sister..."

"Lauren?"

"Yeah, Lauren, the chick that helped you get off on your shit. She made a bad mistake, man."

"Yeah, I'd say she did. What the fuck happened to him, West?" Rossi looked in the direction of the body in the car and swiped his face.

"Rossi, look, her sister left the boy in the hot sun with the windows rolled up and didn't know any better and he died. Shit, she's a good girl and we need to help them out."

"We? Help them outta what?"

"Shit, there's a dead boy here. What do you want me to do, call Stallings? Just help me get rid of the body," I told him flat out. "That's what I need you to help me do."

"Do what?"

"Help me bury him, Rossi. Help me bury the poor little boy."

It took more time than I'd hoped to convince Rossi to help me find a place to bury Lil'Man without the authorities getting involved. Hours. Darkness fell and I took Rossi in to meet Lex. She was broken apart and Rossi decided there was no way she would ever hurt her son intentionally and that's when he finally decided to give me a hand. For his generosity, I told Rossi to keep the twenty thousand Todd left him with because I was determined more than ever to get my share of the three bills back.

I went to the back of my shop. There was a wooded area there beyond a clearing about sixty yards away. It took me a while to dig the grave because placing a dead body in the ground didn't sit too well with me. I kept looking over my shoulder thinking Stallings was somewhere looking at what the hell I was doing. I finished around two that morning. Rossi stayed in the garage with Lauren and Lex waiting for me to give him the word that I was ready while they prayed over Lil'Man.

When it was time to bury the baby, Rossi had to step in and take him away from the girls. We wrapped him up in blankets and placed him in a wooden crate that Rossi secured that was being used to store some of my best motor oil. Lex tried time and time again to stop Rossi from taking Lil'Man away and it became very emotional. I separated Lex from Rossi, then I took Lil'Man and set him where he would rest as Rossi began to cover him with the Georgia red clay.

There was no way Lex could stay with me in my place afterwards. I knew she was hurting and so did Lauren, but she had to go. Things had to definitely cool down. I got a few dollars from Rossi and gave them to Lex. We all decided that the best thing for her to do—was to go back to North Carolina and Rossi took her to the bus station to make sure it happened.

28

The next morning I didn't awake until close to eleven. Rossi stayed over on the couch. Something about the night's events just put him in a dreary mood. Even though I don't think she wanted to hear about it, we managed to fill Lauren in on what happened when Rossi was robbed of our money while we sat around in the kitchen.

"We're going to meet with Stallings tonight. So I need you to be here just in case I have to call you if his ass don't want to deal, okay?" I let Lauren know.

Lauren's voice was dull and attitude straightforward. "If he doesn't want to hear what you got to say, West, what you going to do? You don't have money for a lawyer. And once they get your ass back down in that jail, you know they ain't letting you out."

"Fuck that. I'm not going back to jail. Stallings isn't a fool. Rossi saw Todd kill somebody on tape. I think it's Tammy and I'm sure he wants to know if it is, especially since he trying to pin the shit on me. Talking about he got a witness? He ain't got no damn witness of me doing shit."

Rossi said, "He's right, Lauren. If we don't step to Stallings, that ruthless bastard will stick it to him without thinking twice."

We all froze at the sound of a honking horn down below by my garage. I looked down and it was Mrs. Bullock. Right on time to get her car washed. From where I was standing Mrs. Bullock's car looked just fine. But fine to me wasn't fine to her. She was so prissy at her age and loved to look good. I took Rossi down to wash her car with me. I told him to watch what he said because she was a very powerful woman. He just about hit the roof when he found out how much she paid me to wash her car, plus her ten-dollar tip made fifty bucks in thirty minutes.

"You son of a bitch," Rossi punched at me. I was folding up my money and about to finish drying off Mrs. Bullock's car while she stood close by, ready to get in and cruise.

"What?"

"Fifty dollars to wash this car? You ain't shit," Rossi said out the side of his mouth.

"It's forty. She always gives me a tip."

"I was beginning to think you were cool."

"I am. But I gotta eat, don't I?"

"Remind me when I get older to stay away from your ass."

"Oh, if I see you when we're old and gray, I'll whoop your ass just because." Then I looked over at Mrs. Bullock who had a wide grin on her face. "Mrs. Bullock, you-are-ready-to roll."

"West?"

"Yes, ma'am?"

"I've been hearing knocking in my engine. Can you take a look at it for me?"

"Well, it's going to take me some time. How 'bout I run you home, drive it for a while and tell you what I find out?"

"That's fine."

During the entire ride to Mrs. Bullock's place, Rossi was as quiet as a four-year-old ready to take a nap. When Mrs. Bullock got out the car, he jumped in the front.

"So how much you going to charge her for this?"

"'Bout a hundred."

He looked at me awkwardly.

"For my time, nigga…"

"Your time?"

"That's what I said. Look, I run a business. I got to find out what's wrong with this car, then fix it. I've been driving it for ten minutes already and haven't heard a sound. Have you heard anything?"

"No, nothing."

"That's what I'm saying; I don't even know if I will."

"What're you going to do if you don't find anything—take the engine out?"

"That's right. You damn right and make that paper," I let him know. "This is America, baby, where the name of the game is to provide goods and services and get paid."

Ten minutes later, I pulled over and parked the car.

"What's this? Why are we stopping here?" Rossi asked.

"Need to check something out."

"Like what?"

"Todd lives right up the street."

Rossi became quiet and kept his eyes peeled on the house.

We sat for close to an hour before we noticed a tan conversion van pull up. A white dude, who looked a little too old to be wearing baggy jeans and an oversized Falcons Jersey with spanking new Air Force One sneakers gripping his feet, went up to Todd's door and went inside. He came out after a couple of minutes.

Rossi asked, "What now?"

"Let's see where he goes."

We followed the van for nearly five minutes. He stopped at a corner and as it might have happened thousands of times before, a young black girl jumped in and slammed the door shut as the van began moving again. We stayed behind them until they parked in the lot of a small makeshift park. It was afternoon so not many people were around. There was a man loading his truck on the other side of the park with his fishing gear and a jogger who ran right past us that we never saw again.

"Now what?" Rossi asked.

"I don't know."

"Damn, nigga, do you know anything?"

I clutched onto the steering wheel, wishing it was Rossi's neck. It was the first time a white boy ever said that to me—at least to my face. I was ready to smash Rossi's head in.

"Why you call me that?"

"What?" Rossi was looking out into the park.

"Nigga? Nigga."

"What's wrong with that? You've been calling me nigga since I met you."

"Watch what you say to me now, Rossi. I'm heated and on the verge of fuck'n you up, man."

"For what?" Rossi chuckled.

"And you have the balls to laugh about it? You don't get it, Rossi, you called me nigga."

"So what? What's wrong with that—geez?"

"So my ass. I'm not your nigga."

"But I'm yours?"

"That's right. You *my* nigga. I can say that to you, I have the right—my people say that now, it's our word."

"Those are some fucked rules and regulations, West."

"Fuck the rules. If you remember, I didn't start the game in the first place, nigga."

"Fine."

"It better be fine," I let him know.

We sat around for a few minutes discussing the situation. When I started in with the history of the word and why I didn't want to hear it coming out of Rossi's mouth—he squashed the shit by apologizing and making nice: more than likely to shut my ass up.

Rossi said, "What you think they're in there doing?"

"What else would a grown ass man be doing with a young girl in the back of a van, in the middle of the day? Geometry or some shit?"

"So what we sitting here for? You trying to catch a whiff of what's going down through the window or something?"

"I feel like crashing the party. You got your heat?"

"Oh, yeah," Rossi said. He pulled up his pant leg and his .38-caliber was sitting pretty on his ankle.

I still hadn't given Lauren her pistol back yet and I took it from under my shirt. "Cool, let's go see what type of position they rock'n."

I went to the driver's side, Rossi on the other. I could smell the weed leaking out the van. My side of the van was locked. Evidently big daddy's girl forgot to lock her side because Rossi had it open and was sitting in the front passenger seat taking in their sounds of pleasure. I nodded for him to open my door as quietly as he could and in no time, we were both sitting as low as possible in the front seats while big daddy and his candy rolled around on the flattened back seat humping hard while listening to loud rap music. We sat for a few minutes, then rushed the back of the van straddling the next row of seats while their pants were still down with our pistols raised.

"Having a little lunch, hunh?" Rossi said.

"Who the fuck are you?" Big Daddy wanted to know.

I flinched my pistol at him. "Shut the fuck up. We'll ask the questions."

The young girl tried to cover her body with her arms, then she brought her knees up to her chest.

"Get some clothes on," I told her.

Rossi said, "Wait a minute."

I looked at him.

Rossi asked, "How old are you?"

She said, "Sixteen."

"Yeah, okay, put 'em back on," he instructed.

"Do you mind telling me what the fuck is going on?" Sugar Daddy asked.

"I thought he told you to shut the fuck up?" Rossi turned to me. "Didn't you tell him to shut the fuck up?"

The young girl stood up, turned around and slipped on her thong panties and her jeans. Then she turned to look at us, I guess wondering what was next.

I pointed my pistol at Big Daddy. "What's your name?"

"Fred. Who the fuck are you?'" Fred had his hands covering himself.

"We're the police."

"Can I see a badge or some shit?" Fred asked.

"No, you can't. You're in here with an underage girl and you want to make demands? I ought to shoot your ass right now," I told him.

"Can I leave?" the teenager wanted to know.

Rossi asked, "What's your name?"

"Stacy."

"Well, Stacy, you know you're wrong. Wrong as hell. Wrong as sin. Just up and down, all around wrong. What you're doing now is the main reason I don't want any damn kids. But we're not going to take you in this time. Stay away from these type of mothafuckas, okay?"

She nodded her head and started to leave.

"Wait a minute," I told her. "Fred, you need to apologize to her."

He asked hard, "For what?"

"If he has to tell you, I'm going to shoot you." Rossi pulled back the hammer on his pistol.

Fred disapproved with his looks more than anything else. But the gat in his face made him rethink his attitude. With his hands still covering himself, he said, "Stacy, I'm sorry."

"Sorry for what?" Rossi taunted.

"I'm sorry for bringing you out here and taking advantage of you."

Rossi turned to Stacy.

"Okay, leave and I better not see you around here again."

Stacy slid open the middle door of the van, slammed it shut, and we could hear her run away.

"Stand up," Rossi demanded.

Fred's eyes became enlarged. "That's okay," he said.

"He said get up!" I shouted.

Fred hesitated before he sat up. His eyes expressed some pussy ass embarrassment for some reason. When he was completely to his feet and dropped his hands, I found out why.

Rossi pointed at Fred. "What the fuck is that?"

Fred looked around. "What?"

"What? That thing strapped on you. Don't you have a dick? Why'n the hell you wearing a strap-on dick?" I asked.

"I ain't got to tell you shit," Fred said.

"Oh, if you want to live, you do." I flinched my pistol at him again.

"Okay, look man. I fuck these young girls all the time and they make me cum too fast, so I use this on them to make them cum. I spend good money and weed on these young bitches and it isn't worth it if I don't make 'em cum. I know ya'll been with a few. You know how it is?"

"I haven't," I let him know.

"And I ain't telling you shit, Fred," Rossi snapped. "I should just shoot your ass, right this minute. Out here fucking sixteen-year-old girls with a strap-on penis extension—pervert."

I found some rope in the trunk of Mrs. Bullock's car and we tied Fred up in the back of his van. I drove him forty minutes west on I-20 to a rest stop just outside Alabama while Rossi followed closely behind. I needed to find out everything he knew about Todd and we drank up all his beer while he told us everything we wanted to know. Just like I thought, Todd was a no-good, scheming asshole drug dealer and con who fronted as though he was a man down on his luck slinging newspapers. Fred had bought dope from him for years and told us Todd had young boys deliver papers for him as well as dope and if they were short on any of the accounts, he would have his boys beat their ass.

When we couldn't stand being around Fred any longer, we took his clothes away from him and told him he could get them along with his keys in one of the stalls in the ladies bathroom after we left. That way, we didn't have to worry about him following us.

"You guys aren't cops. Cops wouldn't do this shit," Fred whined.

"Oh, you prefer us to kick your ass?" Rossi asked.

I said, "We're good cops."

"I want to see badge numbers. What're you guys' names?" he demanded before we left the van.

"I'm Captain Stallings."

"And don't worry who the fuck I am because I don't like your pussy ass," Rossi told him.

As we approached my car to drive away, Fred's naked ass ran toward us.

"Captain Stallings, you son of a bitch. You haven't seen the last of me, you fuckin' nigger!"

Before I could even think of what I was going to do to his naked ass, Rossi pulled out his pistol and looked around for witnesses. Then shot Fred in his leg.

"Man, what's your problem, Rossi?"

"West, the white boy called you a nigga and it was in anger—so he deserved it. It's definitely worth shooting a man over, don't you think?"

I wanted to tell Rossi it wasn't worth it but I couldn't—he was already yelling out to Fred as he grimaced in pain.

"Now go get a strap-on leg, too, punk ass."

layboy Rossi wanted to go to his place, pick out some clothes and shower before the meeting with Stallings. I borrowed a white button-down and khakis from his closet. While he showered I spent a couple of minutes with Lauren on the phone, and she was going nonstop about the lack of concern by the father of her child. He told Lauren that if she was looking for a payday she should forget about it, and if she tried to come after him for child support he was leaving the city and would be off someplace where he could never be found.

His comments were something that didn't sit too well with me. Lauren was bearing a lot of pressure that was beginning to bear down on her. The death of her nephew didn't make things any easier and living for the first time in her life away from her sister was hard. I wanted to ease some of the pressure for Lauren. We were almost at the strip joint but I passed the exit and continued north.

"What's up? Where are we going?" Rossi said, looking at the strip joint as we passed it from the highway.

"I need to take care of something."

I pulled out the address from my wallet where the asshole who knocked Lauren up lived to make sure I knew where I was going.

"What other business we need to take care of?" Rossi asked.

"This is personal."

When we arrived at the address, Rossi didn't feel comfortable sitting out in the car alone so he decided to come along. It didn't take much to realize the niggas living in the digs had some serious cash flow. The subdivision of condos smelled of privilege. The powder white stucco that helped to hold the place up didn't have a mark. I could tell it was one of those places that didn't allow kids. What irony. But even still, I heard a kid's voice inside right before I knocked. A cute little biracial girl with golden silky hair tied in braids, no older than five, struggled to open the door. She smiled and said, "Yes?"

"Hey, sweetie. Is Malcom here?" I asked her.

"What're you doing, China?" a man's voice rang.

"Answering the door, Papa. What's it look like?"

The door was snatched even wider and before the man looked at us, he snarled at the little girl and took a long deep breath, then said, "How many times do I have to tell you not to answer the door?"

Without asking, I knew this punk nigga was who I was looking for.

"I dunno," she answered and then ran away screaming at the top of her voice.

Malcom barely looked at us and told us he wasn't buying and began to shut the door.

I put my hand out so that he couldn't. "We're not selling anything."

He looked at my hand like I had a lot of nerve. But he was the hard-on with the biggest balls—so he thought, playing Lauren the way he was. "Well, I'm not interested then," he snapped.

Something about that man just made me want to chew his ass up. Just the way he looked standing in his all-black outfit and platinum jewelry. Glancing him up and down, I truly believed Lauren when she said—she slept with him on a whim. He wasn't her type. He was too up and down— straight like he was trying to keep something in his ass. He was still rocking a fade haircut; I knew it was a fade because I used to have one back in the eighties. He looked like he could've been one of those Wall Street asshole Negroes that corporate America loves to embrace. But I wasn't impressed with his lanky body or toothpick physique. He was brown-skinned and his face was as smooth as a baby's behind with no facial hair. He was soft; and I knew it—I even smelled the baby powder sprinkled on his ass.

I glanced behind him to see who else might be inside and when I didn't see anyone, I grabbed him by his shirt and snatched him outside.

"Oh my, damn," Rossi said. "You almost pulled him out of his shoes, West."

"Hey, man? What's your problem?" Malcom pulled away from me and adjusted his clothes back in place.

"You're my problem," I told him.

"You must have me mistaken for somebody else."

"Your name Malcom?"

"Yeah, so what?"

"No, you're my problem."

"What?"

"That's right. You know Lauren?"

He looked at me, then over at Rossi without answering.

"Well, do you?" Rossi asked him.

"Yeah, I know her. Why?"

"Because I don't like how your skinny ass is play'n her."

He said, "I don't know what you're talking about."

Rossi stepped to him. "I guess we're both about to find out now, aren't we?" Then Rossi looked at me because he didn't have a clue.

I moved closer to him. Homeboy looked like he was in shape but not like he could knuckle-up. I knew I could break him if I had to. "So you don't know what I'm talking 'bout, right?"

"Okay, man, chill," he said. "Who are you—her father or something?"

Rossi began to chuckle and I was a bit embarrassed because I never liked to be the brunt of a joke, so I just took the asshole by the neck.

"Yeah, that's who I am. I'm her daddy. You see the concern in my eyes? That's of a father's concern. My hands will snap your simple ass neck if you don't do right by Lauren." I took my hands down, then put them or Malcom's shoulders nice and soft and then pretended to knock lint from his shirt. "Now, if you don't come correct and talk to me like a man, plain and simple, you're going to get hurt."

Malcom decided he wanted to have a brief stare-down with me. Rossi watched it unfold.

"Look, nigga, I'm gonna tell you this one time. You're gonna take care of the baby, you understand?"

"I'm going to tell you—just like I told her. That baby isn't mine, I told her that. Why doesn't she understand?"

"Baby? Oh geez," Rossi said.

I grabbed him again. "You're a damn lie."

Right before I was going to bust him in the mouth, a lady called his name. Then she opened the door and peeped out. She wasn't bad looking, but not my type. White girl, frame glasses, five three, tight ass, with teeny tiny tits and a short haircut.

"Malcom? Is everything okay, baby?"

"Yeah, yeah, Sylvia, everything's cool. Just talking to a couple of business associates."

She looked at Rossi first and obviously didn't like what she saw because she turned up her nose and did the same shit to me. "Please hurry up. You don't want to keep your daughter waiting, do you?"

I looked over at Rossi, then at the lady, and said, "Can I ask you a question?"

She shrugged her shoulders.

"Are you two married? Please tell me you're not married."

"We're married but are kind of separated and are in the midst of patching things up. Right, Malcom?" Her looks challenged him to say otherwise. "Why all the questions? Who are these thugs?"

Malcom tried to get in our conversation. "Listen, I'll take care of everything," he rushed to say before he tried to push himself and his lady back inside.

"I'm sure you will," I told him. "But I think she should know about this, Malcom. Don't you?"

She was quick. "Know what?"

"A friend of mine is having his child," I sputtered. "But he doesn't want to take care of his responsibility."

"What? Malcom, is this true? Who is the woman?"

"You done fucked up now, Malcom," Rossi told him.

"Having a baby? What woman? Malcom, you assured me that we were patching things up and you hadn't been with anyone since we separated. When did all this happen?"

Malcom didn't know whom to address. He was caught up and in deep, as we watched his wife storm away.

"Look, you'd better do right by Lauren. You got that?" He didn't answer me—and I gave him a few seconds to give me an answer but when he didn't I punched him in the stomach. He tried like hell to catch his wind while he bent over at the knees.

Rossi took one step closer to him. "It's better if you stand up." Rossi patted him on the back and Malcom rose.

"Thanks, man," Malcom barely got out of his mouth over his hacking.

Out of nowhere, Rossi hit Malcom with a nasty karate-like punch near the spot where I popped the gaping asshole. Then he assured him, "No problem. No problem at all."

➤ ➤ ➤

By now we were pressed for time to meet Stallings so I planted my foot down hard on the gas. It was the first time since I had my car back that I pushed her buttons to see if she was truly okay and she withstood the test, shooting south, down I-75 easily over ninety-miles an hour—and Rossi didn't mind one bit as the wind coming in from the sunroof blew in and down on his isometric haircut.

"You know," Rossi said over the wind coming into the car as I drove.

I looked at him quickly, keeping an eye out for poe-poe. "What's that?"

"In my book, you just don't do that type of shit back there if you don't care for someone."

"Well, sometimes things get like that. People come into your life and you start to care, you know?"

Rossi was now looking straight ahead down the road. "I know. Rita's been like the only thing on my mind lately, too. Truth be told, I only tried to screw her over for the money I owed her so I could see her again."

"The old I-owe-you scam."

"That's right."

"Shit still works, don't it?"

"Like a charm. So, I'm on target. You and Lauren are getting serious?"

"I don't know, man. This relationship shit is hell to deal with. Sometimes it's best to keep your mouth shut when you care about someone so they won't burn you in the end. Then again, the ladies want you to *express yourself*—you know, be more open. That Dr. Phil shit. And yet still you could end up gett'n played anyway. All I know, even though I just lost Tammy, I haven't felt this way since I was a young buck doing stupid shit back in the day."

"Yeah, I did some crazy shit back in the day," Rossi reminisced. "Fucking two girls a night. Playing endless mind games to keep the upper hand." I noticed Rossi faintly smile. "Those were the days," he said.

"From what I see on the block—niggas still play'n head games with the ladies."

"Don't seem much like a bad idea though."

"Yeah, but sometimes you gotta give that shit up, Rossi, 'cause it don't mean the same as it used to."

Rossi said, "True that."

"I been thinking though," I told him.

"About?"

"Writ'n a book."

Rossi chuckled at my idea. "A book?"

"You heard me. A book called *Niggas Ain't Shit*."

"Have you lost your fuck'n mind, man?"

"I'm serious."

Rossi lit up a smoke. "Okay, I'll give it a listen. What's the premise?"

"It's about all the niggas who are constantly fuck'n over good women. That's what it's about; nothing more, nothing less."

"So…is this book specific, or in general?"

"What are you talk'n about, Rossi?"

"I'm just saying, because I know a lot of white boys who fuck over women, too."

"So?"

"So, I guess they're niggas too, right?…Right?" I looked over at Rossi while he blew smoke rings. "Like I said, I'm just saying, my brother, I'm just saying."

30

We arrived at Nikki's and I spotted Stallings right away and then walked over to him. Rossi didn't follow me. Instead he waited a few minutes by the door after he told me where he would be sitting. I sat down next to Stallings.

"You think you could'a gotten any closer to the dance floor?"

"You're late," he growled. "Besides, I like close. That way you can see all the nooks and crannies." Stallings flipped a few bills to a dancer who opened wide for him. "When you get placed in the penitentiary, you'll see exactly what I mean when your new boyfriends have you up on a table in a blond wig making you dance for them."

I had grown used to Stallings' punk ass threats and bullshit sarcastic remarks. They didn't bother me one bit. Stallings put a few more dollars on the stage.

"I didn't know cops could do that on duty."

Stallings' look was cold. "I thought you knew? I do what I want, especially after they moved me to homicide. Fuck 'em. What you got for me?"

"Slow down. I want to know about this witness of yours—because it's all bull. I didn't kill Tammy. Why would I?"

"My money says different. I just have to confirm a few items, and you're going to be charged." The grimy, no-good grin Stallings placed on his face made me want to punch him in the mouth.

"Look, I don't know what you have but I didn't kill anyone."

"I have a witness. I'd be a damn fool to give you the name because if you're Tammy's killer you'll probably do them, too. But so far, everything the witness says checks out, but like I say, I just have another item or two to look into."

I challenged him. "Damn it. What checks out?"

"Look, I thought you had something for me?"

"Okay, Stallings, but listen—I didn't kill Tammy."

"Tell me what you have before I haul you off. I'm tired of looking at your sorry ass."

I shook the punk's comments off. "A killer and drug dealer. One and the same."

"Give me a name?"

"His name is Todd." I hesitated because of how quickly Stallings' eyes moved from the dancer to me. "You know him, hunh? He's the dirty muthafucka who did the murder and is slinging drugs. I'm surprised he didn't tell you—when you were over at his place asking about me."

"How do you know?"

I flipped the script on him. "I have witnesses; that's how."

Stallings looked at me with a half-grin. "You listen to me…"

I cut him off. "I have witnesses on the murder and drugs."

"I'm listening."

"Naa, no can do, fuck that. Do I look like a stupid nigga to you, Stallings?"

"I've told you that before."

"Well, I'm not. You of all people should know a nigga needs a deal."

"And how should I know that?"

"'Cause you a nigga and you know a nigga ain't giving shit for free. Them days over."

Stallings exhaled sharply. "Okay, tell me what you want?"

"Immunity."

"Immunity?" he echoed.

"Right."

"You have honestly watched too much HBO or some shit. You have to have done something to get immunity. And if you didn't kill your girlfriend, what do you need it for?"

"Oh, I got some shit for you; that's for damn sure."

Stallings thought for a while. "Tell me what you got?"

"Immunity."

"Okay, shit," Stallings answered. "You got it."

"Immunity for everyone involved with me."

"Damn it, West. You're stretching it."

I pulled a folded eight-and-a-half-by-eleven sheet of paper from my shirt pocket and slid it to him.

"What the fuck is this?"

"My guarantee—I don't trust you." Then I slid our deal on paper toward him. "Sign it. It's all written up."

He began to read. I knew it was only a matter of time. Stallings took his cigar out of his mouth. "Pete Rossi? What the fuck is going on here and how in the hell do you know Pete Rossi?"

"Sign it and you'll find out all about it."

Stallings didn't hesitate to sign after Rossi's name came up and I placed my document safely in my shirt pocket. Then I told Stallings everything, at least everything he needed to know to get the murder rap moving in another direction and hopefully off my ass. I put it on the line and Stallings bit. I told him about the grand jury deal with Rossi, minus Lauren, and when I did, it seemed like the perfect time because a dancer had her ass just inches from his face. I didn't know if his mouth was open because of what I told him or what he saw. After the dancer finished, Stallings wanted proof that I even knew Rossi. Rossi had been watching us from across the club and I nodded my head toward him. When Stallings followed and noticed his former snitch, Rossi gave him the finger, then smiled.

Stallings smiled. It was an embarrassed gesture that was fueled with anger. "You guys ran a smooth game on me. No wonder that mothafucka got off."

"And it's the only thing we have over our heads. I didn't kill Tammy and I want to prove it before you try to pin it on me."

Stallings took another glance at Rossi who was now busy with a dancer. "So you say you know who the killer is?"

"That's what I'm say'n. I know who killed Tammy. But I don't know why and I need time to find out."

"What kind of time you talking, West?"

"Long enough to find out. And stop calling my damn house, man. All that talking about how you're going to lock me up has my people on edge. A nigga can't work like that."

Stallings' look was still. "I'll give you three days."

"Three days?" There was no way in my mind.

"You're right. That's too much time. Make it two."

"What?"

"That's right. Two days. I'm freak'n tired of working homicide. If I can get these cases in a file jacket, I'm sure narcotics will take a nigga back."

I told Stallings not to call me. I would call him when I had something to give him. At least we had a deal now—that alone was enough juice in my system to find our money and the tape of Todd killing Tammy so I could get on with my life.

> > >

Outside the club it was storming to no end. The streets were slick and fog had begun to cover the city. We decided to go to my place to figure out how we were going to deal with Stallings' request of the delivery of Tammy's killer in two days. We weren't five minutes into the drive before I noticed the shining, twirling lights in my rear view mirror. Then a bull-horn demanded that we pull over.

Rossi became excited and began twisting in his seat to see what was going on. "What the fuck you do, West?"

"Nothing."

"Well, what is this then?"

"I bet that punk ass Malcom got the plate number and called us in. Be cool, man, be cool."

I could see one police car behind us. Its lights were flashing violently and were accompanied by an awful continuous blast of a siren. After I pulled over, we sat still waiting for the officer to approach us. Two minutes later another squad car pulled up directly in front of us. Ten seconds later, another.

"Okay, West…What the fuck is this?"

"I don't know—but I'm getting out."

Rossi grabbed my arm. "You wanna get us both killed? Don't do anything. Don't even breathe."

Because I turned the car off when we pulled over, the wicked humidity from the outside began to take over the car making it more difficult to breathe. I looked back through my driver's side mirror and could faintly see through the rain the blue trousers of an officer walking toward the car; they were tucked down into leather boots. Finally, there was a tap at the window. I looked over at Rossi and he agreed with his eyes for me to roll my window down. When I did greet the officer, a leather-gloved fist punished my jaw.

I woke up I don't know how many minutes later with my left wrist hand-cuffed to a chair sitting next to Rossi. His right wrist was cuffed to my chair. I fought off my dizziness as fast as I could, but I was dazed and my jaw was thumping all the way down into my back teeth. We were sitting in a bedroom of a house that was being constructed. I asked Rossi if he was okay but I couldn't get him to talk to me. There was blood dripping from his mouth. I didn't see what had happened to him. But there was no doubt he'd gotten the shit beaten out of him and it wasn't pretty.

The room we were in smelled like piss and days of horrible funky, laid around shit. After my eyes regained their focus, I could read a sign that had been taped to the wall written for the Mexican workers who built ninety-nine percent of the homes in metro Atlanta. "*No pee-pee or khaka in house. One hundred and fifty dollar fine!*" Evidently the mothafuckas couldn't read.

I took my right hand and lightly smacked Rossi on the cheek. "Hey, man. Wake up. Rossi get up." Rossi didn't budge. I heard footsteps walking up the framed steps. Hard steps; it sounded like a platoon of folks making their way to us. I kept my eyes toward the entrance. When the sounds of the footsteps stopped, I could see Stallings and three big-ass sneering cops looking down on us.

Stallings walked over. "My-my-my. If it isn't Mr. Immunity himself."

"Stallings, what the fuck is going on?"

"Shut the fuck up. I don't have time to waste." Stallings motioned to one of the cops and pointed to Rossi. "Wake that piece of crap up."

A big white cop standing at least six-five and two hundred and fifty pounds walked over to Rossi. I knew he must have been the one who hit me because he was the only one with gloves on. He snarled at me, reached into his shirt pocket and pulled out smelling salt. After waving it in front of Rossi a few times, Rossi finally opened his eyes. Stallings barely gave Rossi enough time to get his bearings before he moved back in on us as he paced the floor.

"It smells like shit in here, doesn't it, gentlemen?"

His cops agreed with him. Some even laughed about the unbearable funk.

"And I'm not talking about the shit and piss the fuck'n workers have fucked this house up with. I'm talking about the shit sitting right before me. The two hard-ons who are responsible for me losing my luxurious job in narcotics and all the wonderful perks of drugs that I could get my hands on and put right back on the street anytime I fucking wanted. Gentlemen, these are the two men that put a dent in our drug business and took food from our plates. But they're going to make it right. Yes-the-fuck-they-are." Stallings walked over to me. "Ain't that right?"

I didn't answer right off but Stallings stood silent. When I told him, "Yes," Stallings hit me in the mouth and asked me who the hell told me to speak. After the blow, Rossi looked over at me.

"Leave him alone, Stallings."

Stallings said, "Oh, look who decided to join us."

"He doesn't have a damn thing to do with this. I'm the one who fucked you up. I didn't know you were in so deep on the streets. Maybe I should have, by the way you kept sweating me to hook up that drug deal. But now I know and we can get the money back."

I struggled to say, "I thought we had a deal?"

Stallings walked over to me. "Thanks for reminding me." He snatched our contract out of my pants pocket. "Give me that shit. Do you think in a million years I would let you mothafuckas even think you could walk free and clear on this shit? Fuck that."

"We had a deal, Stallings," I told him.

"Here's the deal, asshole. The deal is this. You get my money back or you two die. How's that for a deal?" Stallings walked over and stood between us with a conquering smile. "Yeah, I think it's a deal." Then he turned, walked away and told the cops to seal the deal for him. And once again the leather gloves were pounding our faces.

31

Those punk cops beat us for another twenty minutes and did it with precision. Their punches were pinpoint and they knew exactly what they were doing. More than likely their experience came from the ass whippings they'd put on suspects to get them to talk or to confess to shit they didn't do. Most of my blows were taken in the midsection. They made me feel like my ribs were broken into little pieces. They beat Rossi near his back toward his kidney. They beat us just enough to hurt for a while but not enough where we couldn't go and find the money and bring it to Stallings like he wanted us to. We made it home and luckily Lauren was there to mend our wounds.

Lauren said, "What happened?" She was going back and forth between Rossi and me.

Rossi said, "What's it look like?"

"I know what it looks like, asshole. Who did it? I mean shit, didn't you fight back?"

"We couldn't. There were too many of them. They held us while their partners beat us. Wasn't a damn thing we could do except take it."

"I gotta piss," Rossi said. "Help me up."

Lauren looked at him. "I just helped you to the toilet. What the fuck is wrong with you?"

Rossi tried to stand.

"Sit down, man. Your body is fuck'n with you," I let him know.

Rossi fell back down to the couch. "Okay, if I piss on your couch, don't blame me."

"West, let's just forget about this whole thing. Forget about the money. It's not worth your life," Lauren pleaded.

"Can't."

"Why not?"

Rossi said, "Stallings gave us two days to get the money from Todd or he promised that he would kill us."

"That dirty bastard," Lauren squealed.

"He ain't nothing but a drug-pushing pimp. He's been stealing drugs and drug money during busts and putting it back on the streets."

"Two days? How the hell does he expect ya'll to find the money in two days?" Lauren wanted to know. "And why doesn't he just go get the money himself—since he's so bad?"

"Because I don't think his dirty ass wants us to find the money. He wants us to fail so he can kill us."

"Well, we gotta do something," Rossi said. "I ain't ready to die." Rossi tried to get up and go to the toilet again. When he realized he couldn't make it, he plopped back down on the couch. "Oh…fuck me."

➤ ➤ ➤

I knew we didn't have much time. But damn it, we needed to rest our bodies. I felt like I had been beaten with bricks all over my body. Rossi sprawled out on my couch and Lauren followed me back into the bedroom with an ice pack.

"I don't think it'll ever be a good time to talk to you about this," Lauren said.

"'Bout what?"

"The baby's father called."

I tried to get a clue by looking at Lauren's expression. I wondered if he'd told her about my little visit. "So what'd he say?"

"Said he was sorry and wanted to be a part of the baby's life."

"He said that?"

"Sure did. Surprising, ain't it?"

"Kinda, but being *a part* of the baby's life means a lot of different things. What does he mean?"

"He wants us to be together, West."

"Be together?"

"That's what he said."

"All of a sudden, hunh?"

"That's what he said."

I wanted to tell Lauren what I found out about him but I held it in. I had a hunch his wife left him for good and his punk ass couldn't stand being alone and was ready to play Lauren on the rebound. "So, how you feel about that?"

"Don't know. I mean I know the baby is going to need a father. At first I was hyped to go at raising my son alone. But, West, I been keeping my eyes on women raising their kids alone and after what happened with Lex and Lil'Man, shit, I'm going to need some help. There's no way I can do it all by myself."

"It's tough—that's what I've been trying to tell you, Lauren."

"So you'd be okay with it if I decide to see if we could work things out? It's for the baby, West."

"What about you though?"

"Me?"

"Yeah, you. Will you be happy? Shit, kids don't grow up in a matter of weeks."

"I know that, silly. I guess I'll have to learn to love him."

"Why would you do that when you're already in love with someone."

"What?"

I smiled. "You heard me. I know you love me, Lauren."

Lauren was silent for a minute, closer to two.

"Don't you love me?" I asked her.

"Yes, I love your ass, West."

"See, I knew it."

"I didn't want to say anything because I really don't know where it came from—you know?"

"Not really."

"Well, my mother always told me that—love starts with flowers, smiles and happy times together. We haven't had those times, West. Shit, we broke and barely eatin' some nights. But I ain't gonna lie, I do love you."

"And I love you, too," I told her.

"Say what?"

"Yes, I love you. At least I'm pretty sure I do. Let me tell you something. When those guys were beating my ass, all I could do was think of when they were going to leave me alone so I could see you again."

"You thought about me while you were getting the shit beat out of you?"

I moved the ice to my ribs. "Funny, ain't it?"

"Unh-unh…That's fuckin' endearing, boo. You 'bout to make me wet up in here."

"So what'd you say? We gonna be an item or what?"

"*We* as in…" Lauren looked at her stomach. "Us three?"

"That's exactly what I mean."

➤ ➤ ➤

I was only able to get a few hours of sleep. Living with the possibility of being killed and taking on a relationship straight up had a brother on edge. I slipped out of the bed without waking Lauren and looked at the clock—already past midnight. I needed a beer.

When I made my way downstairs, Rossi wasn't on the couch and my front door was wide open. My first thought was Captain Stallings' boys had taken him out again to beat on him some more. I grabbed Lauren's 357 and my flashlight and made it down the steps quietly to see what was going on. I had already made up my mind that if it was Stallings and his boys outside my place fucking around, I was going to start popping off rounds in somebody's ass because I wasn't taking another ass beating.

I made it to my garage and flashed the light inside. There was nothing there except my car. I turned around and looked down the street. Everything looked normal. I stood in the darkness and then I heard what sounded like moaning out toward the back where Lil'Man was buried. I clutched my pistol grip extra tight.

I stood still for a moment to get a take on where the sound was coming from. The woods were dense for the first hundred yards or so because I had cut the grass and shrubs back to make my business look as professional as possible the day after I got my billboard sign. When I got to the thick part of the trees, I cocked my pistol and stood as though my feet were in cement. It must have been two or three minutes before I heard the sound again. I pointed my pistol in the direction, then my flashlight. When the light hit my subject, I squinted my eyes to make sure of what I was seeing. It was a naked ass standing with pants down at the ankles. Then I heard a definite slurp and plopping sound right before I saw two sparkling eyes appear in the light from behind the standing naked ass.

"Hey, West."

I called out, "Rita?" Then Rossi turned and twisted his shoulders so I could see his face. "Rossi?"

"Yes, it's us, so don't shoot," Rita said. "Rossi called me over and I thought I'd bring him out here to make him feel better."

I shined the light in Rossi's face and he was smiling ear to ear. "My brother, she does wonders," he boasted.

I dropped my pistol to my side and stormed away, stomping through the brush. How could Rossi think about a blowjob with all the trouble we were in—I needed a drink for sure after the freak show.

➤ ➤ ➤

Lauren was sitting at the kitchen table eating cookies and milk when I got back in.

"What's wrong with you?"

"What you mean?"

"You look frustrated. Where you been?"

"Outside looking for Rossi."

"Where'd he go?"

"Outside, to get some head."

"Hunh?"

"I thought the nigga was in trouble again, but come to find out, he was out back behind the shop, getting head from his girl."

Lauren shot me a disbelieving look. "Shut up, West. Why you wanna lie on the man like that? Talking about he out there getting his dick sucked. You must have taken one too many to the head or something. How foul can you be?"

"Okay. It wasn't happening. Forget about it."

32

Twenty minutes later Rossi came back in with a relieved smile on his nasty face. Rita was standing behind him like it was just another day at the office for her. But she seemed to be proud that she could make Rossi feel so good. Lauren looked at Rita, wondering who she was.

I said, "Lauren, meet Rita. That's what I was talking about."

Rita smiled. "You didn't have to tell her, West. But it's cool. If a woman can't please her man, there's always somebody else who will."

"I heard that," Lauren echoed.

"Oh, so now it's okay when she confirms the shit, hunh?"

Lauren said, "Hush up, West. Ya'll come on and sit down."

There was a deck of cards on the table and Rossi picked them up and began to shuffle them. He shuffled cards like a pro and once he knew he had everybody's attention, his card tricks instantly became professional and they lured us into his world. Rossi enjoyed the attention. He constantly called out our names, one at a time, asking us if we liked what he was doing. Lauren poured everyone a drink, herself another glass of milk and we watched Rossi go through all of his card tricks. Then we paired off and busted some spades for an hour or so before anyone said anything about what we were facing with Stallings.

"Are you guys scared to do something or you honestly don't have a clue as to what you're going to do with your little situation?" Rita asked.

"I was wondering the same thing," Lauren echoed. "Sitting up here playing cards like you don't have a care in the world."

"What can we do? I was thinking about going over Todd's with guns blazing, but the dildo-man we caught coming out of Todd's house—told us he now has more than a few niggas wishing someone would try to get in his place and take his drugs because of the big shipment he just got in."

Rita said, "Oh, a real tough guy? Well, you know what they say about tough guys, don't you?"

I looked up from my hand. "What's that, Rita?"

"Tough guys are straight-up pussies when it comes to pussy."

"You should know," I said.

"You're right. I should. I've dealt with a lot of self-proclaimed bad boys."

"How's that?" Lauren wanted to know.

Rita looked at Lauren, and then glanced at Rossi and me. "What? West didn't tell you?"

"Tell me what?"

"Girl, I make my living on my back. And a good living it is," Rita confessed.

"So, what you say'n, Rita? Just because a nigga gets weak when he about to bust some drawers don't mean a nigga won't bust a cap in your ass," I said.

"Please. It's the way you approach a tough guy."

"I didn't know there was a special way?" Rossi questioned.

"Oh, yeah there is, and I bet Lauren knows all about it—don't you?"

Lauren smiled, looked down in her cards, and said, "Yeah, I know."

"How you know?" I asked.

"'Cause I do."

Rossi asked, "How then?"

"You treat them like their mothers," Lauren told us.

"Tell them, girlfriend," Rita reinforced.

"Make him feel like a little boy again. Talk to him like a fucking sixth-grade punk who still wets his pants from time to time."

"Make him feel like you care about him, when in reality you couldn't give a good fuck about him," Rita added. "One thing about men; they love their mamas. Mamas can do just about anything under the sun to their sons and it doesn't matter to them. You get under a man's skin—like his mama? And you got a controlled punk ass man who you can breast-feed every night."

"Under control," Lauren co-signed.

I looked around the card table. "Now I know ain't nobody up in here think they got a little ass boy up under them?"

"Damn right," Rossi added. "I mean—I'll suck a titty every night if it's put in my face, but don't think I won't kick a skank out if I think she's trying to game me."

"Would ya'll just shut the fuck up?" Lauren said. "You wanted to know; now you know."

"Okay, I hear what you say'n but how the hell is that shit going to help us in our little situation?"

Rita said, "I never told anyone this but I've wanted to open up a child daycare for the longest. Cut me in on the money so I can make it happen and I'll show you a way to get to him."

"So you'd use the money for some good, too?" Lauren questioned.

"That's right. How much longer can I continue to lie on my back? Shit, pussy has its limitations, too, you know."

"Have you all forgotten about Stallings? He wants the money," Rossi reminded.

"Forget Rossi," Rita said. Everyone looked at her. "Why should we give it to him?"

"Because we want to live," Lauren said.

"He's no better than us," Rita said.

I said, "I think Rita's right. Fuck him. We'll figure out how to deal with him when the time comes."

"The time is coming sooner than you think," Rossi said.

"What'll you say? We'd be splitting three hundred grand four ways."

Everyone agreed that we were going to get our money and somehow not give Stallings a cent of it. I definitely needed it for my shop that was quickly going down the tubes; Lauren for her child; Rita for her daycare; and Rossi to more than likely get into more trouble with.

➢ ➢ ➢

I sat and drank the rest of my E&J back with Rossi while we listened to Rita propose a plan. She let us know right off the bat that she would need Lauren's help. That's when Lauren let her know that she was pregnant.

"Wow, girl, you don't look it. All I need you to do is get as fly as possible."

"That's it? Where are we going? What are we gonna do?"

"There's a wine sip at the Hyatt downtown tonight."

"Wine sip?"

"It's supposed to be in the honor of some type of dorky endowment foundation, but it's nothing but a front for some of the biggest drug dealers and wannabes in the city."

"You mean the front they have downtown once a month at the Hyatt?"

"You know about it, West?" Rita asked.

"Yeah, heard all about it."

"How?" Lauren wanted to know.

"Heard about it when I was locked up. Couple of guys were running off at the mouth. Now my question is—what makes you think you can even get in, Rita?"

"One of my clients invited me."

"Oh, really now?" Rossi asked very defensively.

I interrupted Rossi's questioning look. "Look, so what? We go to the wine sip, then what?"

"No, I go, with Lauren," Rita corrected.

Lauren said, "What are we going to do there?"

"We look for Todd and when we spot him, work girl-to-girl magic on him so he'll stick to us like glue."

"Yeah, but first we have to get him there," Rossi reminded.

"Not a problem. I have a friend who owes me a favor and if this Todd is as big a drug dealer as you say, he'll know him and invite him. And I will have my friend introduce us to Todd, then it's up to us to get him back to his place to get the money."

"This sounds too damn easy," Rossi said. "Shit will never work."

"And do you two realize he's already killed once?" I asked them.

Lauren looked at Rita and said, "What else are we going to do? I mean—If you think about it, I'm the one who got us into this in the first place by trying to break Rossi free from his case. I'm going for it."

I looked at Rita. "What about you?"

"Sure, why not? This is for my future and in my line of business—you always take risks."

sat around with Rossi drinking and playing spades while the girls prepared to go out. Rita wasn't lying when she said she knew people. Minutes after agreeing to our plan, we all sat around the table and listened to her phone conversation, convincing some big-baller to contact Todd and invite him to the sip. It was hard to read Rossi's expression (but he was feeling something; I could tell by the way he glanced at her) after she told her *friend* he would never regret introducing her to Todd.

I wasn't as surprised as everyone else when Rita's contact said he'd heard of Todd. I knew he was up to no good the very first time I laid eyes on him. I had a feeling Tammy was looking down at his skinny ass wondering why he would do such a thing to her.

Rossi wanted to go home with Rita so she could change but I talked him out of it. Those two alone meant sex was going to go down and there was no time for that; we needed to let the ladies get ready, then get to the sip and see what the girls could do with Todd. Our clock was ticking and Stallings would be on the prowl the next day.

We followed the girls to the Hyatt, watched them go in, and parked my car around the corner. I was a bit jealous knowing roughneck niggas would be inside the gathering looking my girl up and down. Lauren was looking so good. Her eyes were lined perfectly. The black dress she had on was very kind to her. No way could you tell she was pregnant. Her ass—the way it poked out from the dress—made me want to hurry up and get her back home so I could take it off her. She definitely had a pregnant glow she and Rita were gabbing about.

Rossi couldn't take his eyes off Rita and all the way to the hotel he continued to ask me if I saw how fine she was. (It was becoming apparent he was falling for her.) Then all of sudden, he started to talk about how nice her tits were. I asked him if he knew they were stuffed with gel. He didn't believe me and told me that I was jealous that Lauren's tits weren't as big. I left Rita's tits alone; if Rossi liked them, so did I.

We played it cool. We left the car around the block, and sat across the street from the Hyatt on the front steps of a bank where we had a perfect view of everyone going in and out. Rita was right. It was a wine sip there. A few of the guys I could tell were straight-up dope pushers and buyers because they came in limos and were flossing to the tenth degree. Others were low-key about what they did; they came in their own cars or even cabs, and didn't dress flashy, while constantly looking over their shoulders to see if they were being followed.

"Look at these ass wipes," Rossi said.

"And?"

"They got balls, man. And I have to tell the truth here. I've slung some reefer a time or two." Rossi looked at me.

"Or three," I said to him.

"Whatever. But never enough to where it just pays all the bills—like these guys do."

"They're extreme, no doubt."

Rossi spotted Todd getting out of a Cadillac Escalade SUV. It was black through and through. Rossi couldn't take his eyes off him. I guess the ass beating Todd and his boys put on him began to playback in his mind. Now all we had to do was wait and hope that Lauren and Rita could work him after the introduction and make him believe he was going to take them home and sex them up.

The sip must have been the shit because I kept seeing carloads of fine ass women going inside. One thing about Atlanta, if there was a party with men with money in attendance, the gold diggers were always out in full force. Rossi started to complain that the concrete we were sitting on was hurting his ass. I gave him the keys and he went around the corner for the car. After we sat across the street for a few hours and the bellboys fell back inside the doors, we pulled the car into the oval-shaped parking lot right in front of the hotel but far enough from the door where we wouldn't be noticed.

"So what now?" Rossi asked.

"Just like we planned. We just wait. Hopefully Rita and Lauren get the fool to think he can have them both for the night and when they get his ass ready and relaxed at his place, we'll bust in and get our shit."

"And...kick his ass," Rossi added like he couldn't wait.

We waited for almost another two hours. I dozed off a bit, almost forgetting that possibly in another twenty-four hours I could be looking death square in the face. Rossi nudged me and said the ladies were coming out with punk ass Todd. My vision was a bit sketchy but I could see that Todd had his arms around both the ladies. Rita and Lauren were playing a hell of a role getting him to think he was really "the man" he claimed to be. When the bellhop pulled Todd's vehicle to the front, they all jumped in and our plan was about to go down.

"Keep an eye on this asshole, West," Rossi said.

"Yeah, I got him, man. The girls did their job; now it's time to do ours."

"Looks like he's headed back to his place."

"Exactly what we want," I said.

"Imagine? This punk thinks he's gonna fuck both of them tonight. Now what kind of shit is this?"

"It's a power thing. Bitch thinks he's powerful 'cause he got some dough and drugs—our dough but not for long. Oh, hell no, he ain't play'n us like that."

34

We drove behind Todd at a near distance—never letting more than three cars between us. We didn't want to tip him off that he was being followed but wanted to stay close because he might have had other plans for the girls other than going to his house. When he pulled onto his street, I stayed on the corner and watched them pull into his driveway—then stroll into his house. Then I parked.

"Let's go see what's happening," I said to Rossi right before I took the 357 from up under my seat. I looked over at Rossi who was making sure his pistol had enough shells. "You ready for this shit, man?"

"I have to be, don't I?"

"Damn right 'cause you know it's a good chance one of us could get killed up in this bitch," I admitted.

Rossi said, "Fuck it. I don't see a better reason than dying than that three-hundred grand."

I opened the car door to get out. "My feelings exactly."

There was no way we could jeopardize walking down the street together close to five in the morning toting heat. Talking about an ass whipping from the cops. So Rossi took the short distance to Todd's first. I followed a few minutes later.

I met up with Rossi in the bushes next to a side window. We had the perfect view of Todd's living room and that's where he wanted his freak show with the ladies to go down. There were three of Todd's thugs in the house—more than likely keeping an eye on his stash. When they saw the ladies, they all planted smiles on their horny faces. Rita was standing right next to his big screen television and I noticed her point to Todd's cronies. Todd looked at them and pointed to the door. A few seconds later we found ourselves caught up in the shrubs trying not to be seen as they made their way out to their cars in the driveway.

Rita seemed to be more comfortable with the setting when we peered back through the window. Lauren played things cool but I could tell she was uncomfortable with Todd around her. She was a solider for the cause anyway. I could see Todd beginning to edge the girls on and Rita didn't miss a beat. She pulled her tight-fitting, red, cotton dress over her head in one swoop—and as soon as Todd put on some music she began to do what she did best—entertain. Rita swayed her hips from side to side with complete confidence that she could make Mack Daddy Todd drop his defensive and give us our chance to come in his place and get what we needed.

Rita was on center stage; she took her tits, squeezed them and slowly one after another brought them up to her mouth and dragged her tongue around her nipples. I looked at Lauren and, even in the tight situation, it seemed to me she was wondering how it would feel to have such humongous tits. Rossi nudged me and motioned to Rita with his head as though he was proud. Lauren played it smart. Todd was so amazed by the size of Rita's tits that Lauren took his hands and led them to Rita, keeping the attention away from her as much as she could.

"You ready to join the party?" I whispered.

"Hell yeah, I'm going to give him this pistol to suck on," Rossi growled.

We made sure as far as we could tell no one could see us go to his front door. I didn't know if I could kick the door down myself because it was one of those extra metal doors that you buy from Home Depot. So on three, we peppered it with shots, and then kicked the bitch in and it was on.

I didn't see it through the window but Todd reached for his pistol on top of the big screen and he shot two rounds. One was much too close to my head and the other near Rossi as we both hit the floor and screamed for the girls to get down.

"Oh, you bitches set me up?" Todd realized. Then he pointed his pistol at Lauren as she ran toward me. I punched about three rounds straight for Todd's freaking head so that he didn't have a chance to take a pop at her. Rita ran and put her head down next to Rossi.

"So now what, punk ass?" Rossi said. "You don't have your boys here to back you up and now your ass gotta pay, bitch."

"Is that your punk ass, Rossi? I thought I told you don't be a fool? But I see you didn't listen so now, white boy, you got to get dealt 'wit because you fuckin' with the wrong nigga."

"You got it all backwards," I told him and I shot about three rounds in Todd's direction over Lauren's screams.

Todd said, "So what you mothafuckas goin' to do? Hunh? What you gonna do? Speaking of my boys, that sounds like them now."

I took a glance out the window and it was Todd's crew jumping out of cars and storming the house as though they'd gotten an emergency page or some shit. We pushed the girls' heads down and went directly for Todd and his boys' guns blazing for about forty seconds. At one point the rounds coming at me were too fierce and I moved away from Lauren to stop the rounds from reaching her. When the smoke cleared, we looked up and heard Lauren scream. Somehow, as I moved a few steps away from her through the darkness, Todd and his boys grabbed her and were able to get out of his house and drive off. We stood silent until Rita snapped us out of what had gone wrong.

"C'mon, guys, we gotta get outta here," Rita said.

"Them bastards took Lauren..." Rossi said.

"Son-of-a-bitch."

35

When we got back to my place, Rita was hysterical. All the gun-fire, screaming and the thought of almost being killed shook her up. Rossi tried to calm Rita when it seemed as though she was about to pass out, but it wasn't much he could say to soothe her. I couldn't take much of her wailing and when she wouldn't stop with all of her suspicions of what could have happened to Lauren—I put her in my room and let her lie across the bed. Rossi was fuming mad but very quiet and I had been made even harder and didn't care what I had to do—or who I had to hurt to get Lauren back.

I didn't know what else to do but I had to do something so I went back to Todd's to take a look around while Rossi stayed with Rita. When I got there it was about noon and everything seemed normal around his house with no sight of the police. This time I didn't park my car around the corner. I parked about four houses away on the opposite side of the street. I was at the point of desperation because now those bastards had my girl and son. After I stood on the porch for a few seconds, I looked around and then turned the doorknob to let myself in. I checked to see if I was alone. Then I started to look for the money, the tape of Tammy's murder, anything that would help me find out where he took Lauren. After a few minutes of tearing the place up, I flipped the couch back upright from off the ground and then sat down. My eyes traveled to an ESPN tabloid magazine. The address on the tabloid was not of the house where I was sitting. It was a Decatur address and that's when I remembered Tammy telling me that Todd owned another house there. I had a good feeling he was there with Lauren.

> > >

There was no time to go back and get Rossi. I had to find Lauren. On the way, I tried to retrace everything that I had been through. I realized Todd did have something to do with Tammy's murder. I never told Tammy what I was going to see at the drive-in with Lauren the night we met Rossi like he claimed—the day I went over his house and the movie *Training Day* was playing.

It was midday so the traffic to Decatur wasn't bad. But finding his place was another story altogether. When I arrived in Decatur, that's when I had to piecemeal my way to his address. I stopped at a few gas stations to ask my way around, looking for Brownsmill Road. When I finally made it, I followed the winding road for miles and soon enough I was out amongst the cows and shit. Finally, I found Todd's address and the car that he sped off in with Lauren—it was in the driveway of a two-story brick home; much nicer than the place he had in the city.

I parked on the road, then made my way through the wooded lot toward the house. The vehicle that Lauren was taken away in was the only one parked in the driveway. I went to the back of the house to see if I could get in. The back door was locked and I had to walk all the way back to my car to get my crowbar from the trunk. Right before I stepped out of the wood line to get it, I noticed poe-poe looking inside my car and sticking a ticket on the windshield. It took him forever to finish but after he did, I ran to the car, popped the trunk, grabbed my tool, and ran all the way back to the house.

I popped the back door to the basement. When I stepped inside I understood why Todd's punk ass thought he was the shit. His basement was laid out. Everything inside was top-of-the-line. The basement had four different rooms but there was no one around. The basement door leading upstairs was wide open and I quietly moved up the stairs and was on the first-floor hallway when I reached the top.

I walked into the kitchen and saw Todd's keys. I put them in my pocket and walked around the dining room, living room and a family room. When I looked upstairs—that was when I began to hear voices coming from a room all the way down the hall. It was Lauren's voice.

"You'd better let me go," she demanded.

I wasn't wasting any time. I broke through the door and shot Todd in his leg before he was able to move. I stepped over his punk ass and went to Lauren who was naked with her hands tied to the bed.

Todd screamed in pain.

"Did his punk ass touch you?"

"No, but he was about to. Take these ropes off me, West."

I untied Lauren as quickly as I could. She put on her clothes and shoes, then walked over to Todd and kicked him in the ribs over and over again. I never bothered to stop her.

36

Todd had plastic gloves under his sink and we put them on. I didn't want any prints to link us to being in his house. Todd's refrigerator was full of T-bone steaks and fresh vegetables. I hadn't had a decent meal in days, so I had Lauren take my car down the street to the gas station and call Rossi and Rita. She invited them over for a home-cooked meal.

While Lauren cooked, I retraced my steps and wiped off everything that I'd touched. Then I took a look at Todd's leg, I was right. He was a punk. I only grazed him in the leg. His punk ass bled for a while and I threw him a pillowcase that he tore and used as a wrap. I took the rope he had Lauren tied with and used it on him. While Lauren cooked the steaks, baked potatoes, tossed salad and a lemon cake, I sat Todd on the kitchen floor and tried to reason with him concerning the money and the tape he made when he killed Tammy.

"I'm not telling you shit," Todd said for the umpteenth time. "And I'm not cleaning up this fucking kitchen when you mothafuckas finish eating either."

I popped open one of his expensive bottles of wine and then went over to Todd and punched him in the face. "You might not be able to clean up when I'm finished with you so shut your mouth."

He laughed at me and tried to bear the pain.

"You're going to tell me everything I want to know, punk, or I'm telling you—I'm gonna kill you."

"How you like your steak, West?" Lauren wanted to know. "This stove is nice. I can get your meat exactly how you want it, no problem."

"Bitch, you never had it this good, have you?" Todd lashed out.

I just shook my head at his silliness. Lauren didn't like his words, so she walked over to Todd and poured an entire bottle of wine on his head. She looked up when Rossi and Rita walked into the kitchen. I gave them both a pair of gloves for their hands.

Rossi announced, "Okay, I'm ready to eat, damn it." Then he looked down at Todd. "Look, Rita, here's the pussy that needed four of his friends to hold me down while he stole my money."

Rita moved in on him and said, "He doesn't look like a pussy, Rossi." Then she looked closer in his face. "But he sure smells like a pussy," she admitted to us.

"Fuck you, bitch!" Todd yelled as the wine still dripped from his face. "I haven't forgot that you set me up and I'm gonna fuck you up."

Rita looked around at all of us, shook her head and smiled, and then she took off one of her pointed high-heel boots and popped Todd in the head with it.

"Ouch!" Rossi said.

I didn't want to look at Todd while I enjoyed his food, so I stuffed him in a dark closet that sat right off the kitchen. As always, Lauren's cooking was all that. My steak was medium rare, the salad was just right, and my baked potato melted in my mouth. We all ate until we were stuffed. I didn't have any room for cake.

"Okay, it's time to find out where the money and tape are. We only have about eight more hours before we're supposed to meet with Stallings," I let everyone know.

"I thought you said we weren't going to give him the money?" Rossi asked.

"We're not. But we gotta act like we're going to try."

"You gotta plan to deal with Stallings?" Rossi wanted to know.

I smiled and nodded my head.

"Well, let's stop wasting time and take skinny-boy down into the basement and make him tell us where the money is."

➤ ➤ ➤

Rossi beat Todd so bad that, in a matter of minutes, Todd told us where everything was.

Rossi took the money and went to count it with Rita and Lauren in the kitchen while I stayed in Todd's room to watch the tape. Todd's equipment was so elaborate I figured out how to make a copy of the tape while watching at the same time. I knew the girl in the tape was Tammy as soon as I heard her voice. Todd was careful not to show her face but not careful enough to hide the tattoo of a tiger on her ankle that she had done when she was a senior in high school.

I hadn't really grieved until I saw the tape of Tammy in bed with Todd. I don't know if I was hurt because she had the nerve to fuck around on me, or the fact that I saw her take her last breath when Todd's punk ass strangled her after the rape. When I came down to the kitchen, the money had been counted. There was two hundred and forty thousand left. Todd confessed that he had to pay off the thugs who helped him lift the money from Rossi.

Everyone wondered what was next.

"Rossi, take the girls and the money with you over to Rita's. No one will look for us there and we can think of our next move," I told them.

Lauren seemed a little worried. "What are you goin' to do, West?"

"I'm going to stay here and talk to this bitch-ass nigga for a minute."

"About what, nigga?" Todd wanted to know.

Rossi hit him in the jaw. "I guess you'll find out when we leave, won't you?"

37

Todd was pitiful. I was sure he'd been crying when we had him stuffed in the closet while we ate our meal. But I had no time for mercy and, at the time, I definitely didn't feel like he deserved any after watching the tape.

"What're you goin' to do with me, man?" he pleaded. "Why the fuck are you staring at me like that?"

"Shut your whining up," I told him. "I'm trying to understand why the hell you would kill Tammy. She never did anything but trust your crooked ass."

Todd didn't have an answer for me.

"So you killed her for the hell of it? Was it all fun and games or what?" His silence was pissing me off so I pulled my pistol from the small of my back and pointed it directly at his head.

"C'mon, man, it doesn't have to go down like this," he pleaded.

"It's too late now. You should've thought about the consequences before you killed her. Now I have your dirt on my hands and there's no way I'm going down for her murder and to be quite frank...you need to be dealt with."

"You have the tape. Turn me in. I'll do the time, fuck it," Todd pleaded.

"Time? Nigga, that's too easy. There is principle behind all this, so tell me why you had to kill her?"

He wouldn't open his mouth. I pushed my pistol into the side of his head.

He said, "Okay, okay. Look."

"I'm listening."

"It never was about Tammy. It was about you, man, and what was about to go down. She told me that you were about to do something big; so one night I followed you to the drive-in over on Moreland. That's when I saw the white boy get in your car. Then I followed him home, then downtown that Monday and figured the shit out. So it wasn't about Tammy. It was about the paper and scoring big time. Nigga, that's all it was. I swear to you."

"Why did you have to kill her?"

"It was a mistake. A stupid mistake, man, I don't know. I didn't plan to. My head got big behind all that was happening. C'mon, man, let a nigga live."

I had to rewind a bit. "So you come into my house, fuck my girl, steal my money, then kill my girl and call it all a mistake?"

"I'm telling you that's what it was," Todd admitted. "A scam. Look, I didn't mean to kill Tammy or take your money, man. Like I say, it was all a mistake. C'mon, man, I want to live..."

I thought about what he said to me, and then dropped my heat to my side. "Okay, fine. I won't kill you for all those things," I decided.

I could feel and see the relief in Todd's face. He even began to breathe easier as he made his way off his knees and said, "Thank you, West. Man, thank you." He wiped his face from the few punk ass tears he shed. "Look, this doesn't have to go any further than..."

I cut him off. "But I will kill you for stealing my car, mothafucka."

➤ ➤ ➤

I made sure there wasn't anything left in Todd's house that could link me to killing him. I left a copy of the tape of Todd killing Tammy on Todd's chest. If things didn't go right with Stallings, then the copy of the tape would at least get me off the hook with the police for Tammy's murder.

I drove away with every last window in my car down. I needed fresh air. I never dreamed everything happening was because we tried to make a little money in the first place. I didn't know how I should've felt about shooting Todd but I grew up on—if someone messed with yours, you do the same to them, no matter what. That's exactly what I did. I didn't feel good about it, but more than likely I would have taken Tammy to be my wife even though we had issues. We weren't exactly madly in love, but we were together and, for that, I felt like I had to revenge her death. Todd killing Tammy was something he did for fun. I killed him because it's all about an eye for an eye in my book. I would have done the same for Lauren if I had to.

➤ ➤ ➤

Lauren was sleep on the couch at Rita's when I got there. Rita and Rossi were in her room. There was no question—what those two were doing but I needed to talk to Rossi, so I knocked on the door. I tapped on the door three times before I called out for Rossi.

"West, that you?"

"C'mon out. I need to talk."

"It's open. Come in, brother. It's cool," he said.

I opened the door slowly, just slow enough to give them both a chance to straighten up. I guess I wasn't slow enough because once again I spotted Rita pulling her head from up under the covers. Either Rita gave the best head in the world and Rossi couldn't get enough of it or she had a serious "Jones" for the dick in her mouth.

"Look, we need to talk." I tried to not look at the coy look on Rita's face.

"What happened to Todd?" Rita pried.

Rossi was quick. "Never mind that. Fuck that faggot. What's next, West?"

"I realized that a man as powerful as Stallings must have a bunch of skeletons in his closet."

Rita interrupted, "Who doesn't?"

"And we need to find out how we can use them against him."

"But how? We only have a few hours until you're supposed to give him the money," Rossi asked.

"I gotta idea. C'mon, Rossi, get your shit. Let's go."

38

came to the conclusion that if anyone knew how to get dirt on anybody who sat on Atlanta's "Who's Who List" it was Mrs. Bullock. All the shit I'd gotten myself into had prevented a brother from thinking clearly. Mrs. Bullock was perfect. Her late husband had been deep into Atlanta politics for over forty years. He was responsible for the last six mayors being elected on his endorsement alone and knew everyone in city government. And Mrs. Bullock, bless her soul, knew everyone in the Rolodex he left behind. Mrs. Shirley Bullock was my answer; from time to time she had a tendency to mention the highfalutin' bigwigs that she kept in contact with who would do anything for her. My plan was to see if she would run a check on Captain Stallings to see what we could find on him. I didn't know if I could convince her since I never had asked for any favors on such a level, but she was my last hope. Stallings was waiting for the money and I knew if we weren't there to give it to him, he was going to have his dogs on the streets looking for us and out for the kill.

When we finally arrived at Mrs. Bullock's place, she was seconds away from mounting a riding mower to cut her lawn. When she noticed my car she walked over to us and we stepped out the car to greet her.

"Mrs. Bullock, why didn't you call me? You know you shouldn't be out here cutting grass."

My concern put a smile on her face. She said, "I know but it needs to be done. The young boy that usually cuts it has gone off on a trip for a week or so," she explained. "And I like to keep things looking nice."

"Mrs. Bullock, this is Rossi."

Mrs. Bullock put a smile on her face. "How-you-do?"

I pushed him toward the mower. "Look, don't worry. He'll take care of your lawn for you. Don't you worry one bit."

Rossi looked at me with a *what the fuck is your problem* question plastered all over his face. Then he smiled down at Mrs. Bullock when we were both waiting for him to get started.

"Oh, thank you, son, you're such a nice young man."

"But I..." Rossi stammered.

"Rossi, we're go'n in the house for a minute. Let me know when you're finished." When I walked away with Mrs. Bullock, I looked back at Rossi and the middle finger he gave me.

Mrs. Bullock kept her house dust free. I thought it was amazing since I had never seen anyone there helping with the estate; maybe having so much time on her hands allowed her to clean all the time. Mrs. Bullock brought some ice-cold sweet tea into the library and we sat in her leather chairs next to the window and watched Rossi work.

She said, "West?"

"Yes, ma'am?"

"I don't think that white boy knows what he's doin' on my riding mower."

I tried to soothe her worries a bit, even though he was running all over her flowers, hedges, shrubs and shit. "Oh, that man has cut many lawns in his day. Even used to work with his father a few years back."

"Well, if he cuts down another one of my plants, I'm gonna go out there and tell him to get his sorry tail off my mower."

"Yes, ma'am, he'll be just fine."

"So what brings you over?"

"Well, I need a favor. And you know I wouldn't come to you if it wasn't important because I don't like to put things on you. I just like to help you out."

"I know, I know. I appreciate you taking care of my car so well. By the way, I've been by your shop the last few days to get a wash but you're never around."

"That's what I want to talk to you about."

"About my car? Something is wrong. I knew it was pulling to the left a bit too much."

"No, no. I want to talk to you about the reason I haven't been around. Maybe you can help me."

"What's the problem?"

I looked out the window before I answered her and hoped like hell Rossi didn't run over the patch of roses he was nearing. When he maneuvered around them, I turned back to Mrs. Bullock. "I done got myself in a bit of trouble, Mrs. Bullock."

"We all do from time to time, son. How can I help you?"

"Well, I need you to use your influence to find out some information for me. You see, my girlfriend and I..."

Mrs. Bullock put a smile on her face. "You mean that cute little thing you got staying with you now?"

I smiled. "Yes, ma'am."

"Oh, she's a keeper, West. You do right by her; you hear me?"

"I'll try my best."

"So how can my influence help you?"

"Well, my girlfriend and I ran into some money that we were going to use to do good with, Mrs. Bullock. I planned to get my shop fixed up and hire a worker or two in the community to be of service. And she wants to open herself a business. But there is a man..."

"A man?"

I took a sip of my tea. "Yeah, a very powerful man who wants to take the money from us."

"Take your money?"

"That's right."

"Why?"

"Because he has the power to do it, I guess."

I watched Mrs. Bullock take a few sips of her tea.

"See, one thing about this city, West, these men in this city are possessed with power and think they can just run over anybody these days. It wasn't like that much when my husband was around. He made sure things ran straight around here."

"And that's why I came to you. I knew you wouldn't appreciate it and would more than likely give me a hand on finding out something about this powerful man, so he can leave me and mine the hell alone and we can get along with our lives."

Mrs. Bullock sat up in her chair and leaned forward. "What's the cocksucker's name?"

➤ ➤ ➤

Mrs. Bullock excused herself and went into her late husband's office just off the library. They had done all right for themselves and I could barely imagine a woman so petite with so many years on her living in such a big house all by herself. Maybe living among the elite was the keeper for her along with over fifty years of her husband's memories because she could have easily moved to a smaller place that didn't take so much time to maintain. Just the thought of her attempting to cut her grass at her age put chills down my spine.

The sound of Rossi on the mower caught my eye when he made his way toward the side of the house where the library was located. I stood up and on his next passing, caught his eye and opened the window to see how he was doing. My man was pissed. He was hot, sweating like he had been out there much longer than twenty minutes and very hard to convince that he should go ahead and knock out the back yard while I tend to business with Mrs. Bullock. Rossi noticed the ice-cold sweet tea through the window, demanded some of it and drank three glasses straight down while he complained about his allergies and watering eyes. Rossi was always on the take. He talked me into giving him an extra thousand dollars out of our money for cutting her grass. Fuck. And he had the nerve to bust my chops for charging Mrs. Bullock to wash her car? He was no different than me, just no damn good at all.

Rossi finally finished the back yard and Mrs. Bullock still hadn't appeared from the office. Rossi wanted more tea but settled for ice water and sat his sweaty self on the floor next to the door. I sat in a chair and was close to falling asleep when Mrs. Bullock finally appeared again.

"Sorry about that but, boy, what a time I had finding out about this Stallings character. Some of my contacts were afraid to spill the beans on him, and others were more than happy to tell me what this bastard has been up to." Mrs. Bullock went to her liquor cabinet and Rossi's eyes lit up. We sat up from our comfort and gave her our complete attention.

"This man is completely trash, I tell you," Mrs. Bullock rationalized. "I don't know how in the world the chief of police has let this man stay on the force for so long."

"Lotta baggage, hunh?" I mentioned.

"Amtrak wouldn't let him ride. I tell you that," she admitted. "This man has managed to dodge plenty of bullets and accusations over his twenty-five years of so-called service. Unbelievable."

"Like what?" Rossi asked.

"Like extortion, shake-downs, prostitution, drugs, murders. Anyone for a drink?"

"I'd like whiskey," I told her.

"Make mine a double, please," Rossi said.

"Well, West, it looks like you got yourself involved with a real son-of-a-bitch."

Rossi stood up and moved over toward Mrs. Bullock. "How do we get next to him though? I mean he gave us a deadline to get him the money."

"Mrs. Bullock, we need something that is still fresh, something still blow'n in the air that he's concerned is about to be put in his face."

"Good idea, West," she offered.

"You got anything like that?"

Rossi picked up our drinks. Mrs. Bullock took a sip of her white wine, then put her reading glasses back on and began to look at some of the notes she had written down. "Here's something. There's a young lady and her mother who recently brought charges against Stallings, and it has pissed off the police chief something terrible."

"What kind of charges?"

"Well, it seems that Stallings was in business with the young girl's boyfriend. The complaint said that he had the young boy selling that crazy crack concoction on Old National Highway for the past two years."

"What a ruthless mothafucka," Rossi said.

"That's just the beginning. It seems that he didn't pay this young man for months and when the young man asked Stallings for his money, Stallings gets upset, and one night bursts into his apartment while this young girl was there. Apparently she's the young man's girlfriend and she is raped by two of Stallings' men while the boy sits by and is forced to watch. Then they threaten to kill them both if they say one word about the incident. And to top it off, they rob the young man of all the money he had in his pockets."

"How come he's not in prison for that?" I wanted to know.

She said, "That's the kicker. The men orally raped her. No evidence of the act."

"So the police chief is pissed behind this, hunh?"

"Yes, indeed, and many others to be exact."

"Yo, Stallings is petrified of the police chief. I know that much," Rossi said.

"Maybe it's your ticket," Mrs. Bullock said.

39

When we got back to Rita's, the front room where we'd all normally sit and shoot the shit was deserted. I could hear the girls though. They were in Rita's bedroom.

We heard Lauren say, "And Rossi doesn't seem to mind they aren't real?"

"I don't even think he knows." Rita chuckled. "At least he's never asked."

Rossi turned to me with his hands raised and eyes squinted. We stood silent and listened.

"Rossi likes nipples too much to be concerned with what's on the inside of these. I had the best surgeon in the country fill me up. Go 'head, touch my tits, Lauren. See for yourself," Rita urged.

"Girl…? I ain't touchin' your stuff."

"Believe me, you wouldn't be the first woman to touch me."

"Are you serious?" Lauren gasped.

"No, some of my girls in my business always want to touch them when they find out they aren't real."

"Oh, I was getting ready to say…"

Rita blushed. "But there was that time about a year ago when me and an associate got a bit too friendly."

"Now that's too much information for me, Rita." Lauren giggled.

"Lauren, go ahead. Squeeze 'em—you'll be surprised how they feel."

Hearing the ladies got the best of me and I wanted to see what was happening. Lauren touching tits? I didn't want to miss it, so I walked into the room with Rossi closely behind me, hoping to catch her in the act.

"Sup, ladies?" I said with a grin on my face.

"Hey!" Lauren said.

"So, what's going on?"

"Nothing much," Lauren said.

Rossi sounded disappointed. "Rita, how come you ain't tell me your tits weren't real?"

Rita looked at Lauren, then back at Rossi and said, "What are you talking about, baby?"

"We heard everything you said out there. You mean to tell me those tits ain't real?"

Rita looked down at them, still proud of her gel packs. "No, they're not. But it doesn't matter 'cause you never had a problem with them—right?"

Rossi walked out the room and said, "Man, my girl got fake tits. Fake damn tits."

Rita opened her shirt. "So what? West, do these look fake to you?" Rita's line of work really opened her up and she must have forgotten I'd already seen them up close and personal. I was hoping like hell she didn't let the cat out the bag and let Lauren know our little secret. I took one quick glance. "I can't tell."

Rita said, "Well, bring your ass over here and touch them."

"What?"

"You heard me."

Rossi came back into the room when he heard her request and waited for my decision with Lauren. Rossi was into Rita too much for me to touch his girl and there was no way I was going to disrespect Lauren like that.

"Look, I ain't come back here to touch on your tits, Rita. We have business to take care of. So let's get down to it."

Lauren and Rossi both agreed with my decision.

➤ ➤ ➤

We explained to the girls what we found out about Stallings and decided that we had to turn the tables on him. There wasn't enough time to go find the young buck he had slinging dope for him or the girl that was raped in Stallings' presence, then to get them to go to the chief of police about Stallings. So we decided to represent them both ourselves, and put Stallings in a bind so that he would just leave us the hell alone.

I didn't want her to, but after we came up with a strategy to deal with Stallings for once and for all, Lauren decided that she would stand in as the mother of the raped girl because our intentions were to call Stallings and let him know that the girl's mother wanted money for her daughter's trouble. We gave Lauren all the information that Mrs. Bullock gave to us concerning the incident so that Stallings would know we were legit. Our asking price would be one hundred and fifty grand more than what Stallings said I owed him. We decided to up the price of the money after we found out how dirty Stallings was.

Lauren was cool and collected when we made the call to Stallings at a private phone booth around the corner from Rita's. As she talked to Stallings, I was rubbing on her belly and our baby.

"Hello, Captain Stallings?"

I could hear the grumpy hump through the phone. "Yeah? Who's this?"

"Mrs. Isaac. My daughter's name is Shay. I'm sure you know her."

"Shay? I don't know any damn Shay," Stallings snapped.

"Okay, the price just went up another fifty thousand," Lauren told him.

"What the hell are you talking about?" Stallings insisted.

"Okay, for that outburst, another twenty-five grand. You're making it very difficult for me to forget about that foul shit you stood by and watched your men do to my daughter."

Stallings was quiet for a few beats. It was like I could hear his heart start to pound through the phone line.

"I want you to know my family is thinking about filing a report..."

"You wait one second..."

"No, bastard, you wait. If you want this little problem of yours to go away, money gets it done—three hundred and seventy-five grand."

Stallings barked. "What are you..."

Lauren cut him off. "I want you to meet me at the Shark Bar downtown in an hour. Bring the money or you'll see your face all over the six o'clock news and that I promise you."

"How am I going to get that type of money?"

"I don't give a damn how you get it. But if you don't, you're going to wish you had."

Lauren and I stood silent in the booth for close to five minutes. I gave Rossi a confirming look as he and Rita sat by in Lauren's car. Then I picked up the phone. It was my turn to give Stallings a call.

"Yeah?"

"It's me, West."

"Well, it's about time," Stallings said. "You got my money?"

"Yeah, I got it. Now what?"

"Bring it to me."

"Fuck that, no dice."

"What?"

"You heard me, man. I don't trust you. The money is in the trunk of my caddy at the All-Star parking lot across from the Dome. It's a…"

"You left three-hundred grand in the back of your trunk?"

"No two-forty. That's how much was left when we finally got it back. You'd better hurry up and take your ass out there and get it," I told him.

"Fuck!" Stallings shouted.

"No, fuck you, and that concludes our business, asshole," I told him.

"What color is your car?"

"You'll know it when you see it."

"What?"

"A diamond is in the back."

40

We drove Rita over to a sports bar that was an eye's view of the parking lot where my car would be with the money. Rita was to call us as soon as Stallings picked up the cash; we knew if he was smart he would use that money to pay the young girl's mother who, in reality, would be Lauren with her hand out. We took Lauren over to the Shark Bar and were sitting in a nearby parking lot.

"Okay, you know what to say to this jerk-off, right?" I asked Lauren.

Lauren was cool. I guess everything that we'd been through had hardened her a bit and it turned me on. "Yeah, I'll take the money, wait a couple of minutes after he leaves, then walk into the parking lot and get in the car with you guys."

"And we'll go pick Rita up and have one hell of a party tonight," Rossi clarified.

Rossi's cell rang. It was Rita. Stallings had the money.

Lauren took a deep breath. "Well, I guess I'll see you two in a few minutes."

I calmed Lauren a bit. "Just remember he's never met the mother before. You don't have anything to worry about."

"Are you positive about that, West?"

"Sure, baby girl. Mrs. Bullock told me—her mother lives miles away and probably doesn't even know her daughter was raped. Just ask him for the money—and we'll be out here waiting for you."

"Got it." Lauren kissed me on the cheek and was off.

Lauren walked into the restaurant. Her steps were hard and quick; there was no hiding she was pregnant. At that moment, I felt closer to her. It hit me that we were truly delving into some true Bonnie and Clyde shit. All the time we spent sitting next to one another on jury duty silent was beginning to add up to vibes that I couldn't explain. I did like feeling good about her though. She was special. Not a bad girl at all. What we were doing was all for good. I wanted her to wait a few more minutes before she went inside, but Lauren wanted to get a bite to eat while she waited for Stallings to show up.

"You know, I'm going to miss your black ass when we're finished here," Rossi said.

"Yeah, right—mothafucka."

"Serious, man. At first, I thought you was some kind of sucker ass, wannabe thug or something. But when I see you around Lauren, you're different."

"Different?"

"Yeah. You care about shit. You are on some compassionate shit with her right about now."

"What?"

"You ask a hundred questions just to make sure she's okay. Like my father before he died, he used to do the same thing to my mother. When you do that type of shit, it means you care."

"Well, I do care about her. And that's straight up."

➤ ➤ ➤

Rossi spotted Stallings going in while he was talking on the phone to Rita.

Stallings ducked into the Shark Bar with the quickness. He had on a dark suit with a matching hat and a nice travel bag that looked like it could hold about three hundred and seventy-five grand in it.

"Cool. Shouldn't take his ass no longer than a couple of minutes to give her the money, then another couple for her to make it out after he leaves," I estimated.

"Make sure you watch that mothafucka when he walks outta there, West. Stallings is a sneaky bitch."

"I got him." I pulled a Tommy machine gun from under the seat.

"Hot damn. Hot damn. Hot damn. Where in the fuck did you get that?"

"Todd."

"Did you bring me one?"

"Under your seat."

Rossi put his hand under the front seat. "My…mothafuckin' nigga! That's what I'm talkin' about." Then he was silent as I looked over at him out the corner of my eye. I think he was waiting for me to blow.

"It's cool. We niggas. We are definitely niggas." I gave him a pound.

"Damn right," Rossi verified.

Then we locked and loaded and put our game faces on.

Stallings strolled out the Shark Bar without the bag. Lauren called Rossi on his phone just to make sure it was safe to come out; we had scored. When we saw Stallings speed away, we told Lauren to come out to the car with the loot. Lauren was sort of hesitant leaving out the door but once our eyes met, she kept them on me and began to move in our direction. All of a sudden she stopped and turned around as though someone had called her name.

Rossi tried to get a better look and said, "Is that…?"

"What the fuck is she doing here? I thought you took Lex to the bus station, man?"

"I did. Who's that dirty bird next to her with the limp?"

"That's Preach, her crackhead friend. I had to shoot his ass a while back."

I yelled out to Lauren who seemed happy to see Lex but mad as hell she was with the crackhead again. "Lauren, c'mon, we gotta go!"

Lauren motioned to me with her hand; one second.

"Lauren, let's go—now."

As soon as Lauren began to walk away, that fuck'n crackhead grabbed the bag on her shoulder and began to pull at it.

I jumped out the car and began to run toward them, but when my feet hit the pavement there were no fewer than seven police cars with sirens and screeching tires headed toward Lauren and Preach tugging at the bag. I hit the ground when the rapid gunshots began to fill the air. I looked up as Lauren tried to run to get out of harm's way, but she fell to the ground and Preach picked up the bag. All of a sudden a police officer hit Preach with the butt of his weapon in the face and snatched the bag and the police detail sped off. Rossi managed to get off a few shots as the police left the scene but they only peppered the cars as they drove away.

➤ ➤ ➤

The hospital was only a block away. We drove there and I carried Lauren inside to the emergency room and stood waiting for help; I couldn't get any help, even though there were doctors and nurses standing in what seemed like amazement of our situation. Lauren was bleeding nonstop and wouldn't answer me. I couldn't understand why no one would come to her aid. Rossi came in a few seconds afterwards and when they discovered he was with us—they finally began to move toward us.

They weren't moving fast enough for Rossi. "Hey," Rossi said. "What the fuck is wrong with you people? Get your ass over here and take care of my friend!"

A police officer approached us and advised Rossi to calm down. He wanted to know what happened. I told him we were coming out of the Shark Bar and were robbed. When the doctors took Lauren from me, I knew it was bad and felt terrible about what had happened to her.

My first thought was that I had more than likely gotten her killed by letting her get the money from Stallings. First it was Tammy—now Lauren. Rossi sat with me in the emergency room. We were trying our best to calm each other down. Rita took a cab to the hospital and joined us on the couch. We all fell asleep waiting on word about Lauren.

➤ ➤ ➤

The next morning at the hospital we were all stacked like leaning dominos on the couch in the waiting room. The doctor that took Lauren from my arms cleared his throat to get our attention.

He said, "Sorry, but I didn't get your names last night?"

I did the introductions and he sat down next to us.

"So, how's Lauren?" Rita asked.

"Well, she's fine," he said. "It was touch and go for a moment but she's really strong."

I heard his words but his face was telling me something entirely different. "But?"

"But, her baby didn't make it," he said. "There was nothing I could do to save it."

41

Lauren spent six long weeks in the hospital and I was completely out of it. I told Lauren how sorry I was and even though she didn't think it was my fault, I felt responsible for her being hurt and losing the baby. The first time I saw Lauren hooked up to all those machines and shit in the hospital I decided right then and there that Stallings was much too powerful to fuck with anymore. I wanted to truly hurt him for having his men jack Lauren and almost take her life.

Out of all the people in the world, Lex came by to see Lauren when she was in the hospital and I'll be dammed if she wasn't high on crack. When Lauren saw her, she barely noticed who she was and I had to ask Lex to leave because she was truly breaking Lauren's heart to see her that way. Lex told me as she was leaving the hospital to tell Lauren that she was going to stop using, but right now she just needed to be high because she missed Lil'Man so much.

Rossi and I had talked maybe three or four times since Lauren had been in the hospital. There was just nothing we could do; we decided that we needed to just move on. Since we couldn't make it together, we just decided to make it on our own. I opened my garage back up full-time and did the best I could while I guess Rossi went back to what he did best. I kind of hoped he was still with Rita. She seemed to care about him. They stopped over the night Lauren came home from the hospital and we were all at my kitchen table playing a game of spades. Everyone except Lauren was pretty much full off the liquor Rossi had brought over. That's when the phone rang.

"West?"

I looked at my watch. It was damn near one in the morning. "Mrs. Bullock?"

"Can you come see me, son?"

"Come see you?"

"Yes, right away."

"Now? Mrs. Bullock, I'm…" I looked into the phone after it went dead.

➤ ➤ ➤

I asked Rossi to ride with me after Rita decided that she wanted to talk to Lauren for a while. We pulled up into Mrs. Bullock's about thirty minutes later. The light in the library was on. We knocked on the door and she let us in and led us into the library.

"Help yourself if you want something to drink."

Rossi was already trashed but said, "Don't mind if I do."

I followed Mrs. Bullock over to her couch and sat down next to her. She must have read the concern on my face. "I'm okay," she let me know.

"You sure? I mean what's the deal calling us out here this time of night?"

"I need to ask you something."

"Okay. What is it?"

"You know I don't do too much of nothing these days, West. But I've been thinking."

"What about?"

"About the shootout on Peachtree weeks ago. I heard a woman was shot there and I have a very reliable contact who told me that Stallings promised some corrupt cops money to carry out a hit the same day as the shooting on Peachtree. But he has refused to pay them, so Stallings has a few of the men ready to turn him in."

Mrs. Bullock was cool and was a big help, when I needed it. But I wasn't giving out any information. "So, is that right?" I asked her. Rossi looked at me concerned while he made his drink.

"Was it your girlfriend, West?" she asked gingerly.

"Mrs. Bullock…"

"Was it…?"

Something told me she all ready knew and wanted to see if I would tell her the truth. "Okay, yes, she was."

Rossi finished making his drink and sat down across from us. "And Stallings killed her unborn baby and almost killed her, too," he said.

"That's what I thought," Mrs. Bullock rationalized.

"That's all you wanted to know?" I asked her.

"No. I called you over to see if you would like to make some money. Big money."

"Money?"

"Doing what?" Rossi asked.

It almost hurt Mrs. Bullock to get the words out of her mouth. But she did. "Killing Captain Stallings."

➤ ➤ ➤

After a couple of drinks and close to four in the morning, we found out that killing Captain Stallings was not Mrs. Shirley Bullock's idea. The people who *really* ran Atlanta presented it to her for us to carry out.

"You mean the mayor?" Rossi asked. "The mayor put out a hit?"

"No. The mayor doesn't have any power in this town. That position never has. It's the reason my husband never ran. Power is never out in front of the masses," she schooled.

Mrs. Bullock was right. As long as I could remember, it always seemed as though there were many background personalities getting mayors elected and giving them their marching orders. Pulling puppet strings. Mrs. Bullock told us some very rich shirt and ties, who didn't care to be named, didn't want the current mayor—who they'd worked like hell to get elected—to begin to take the onslaught of the media if and when all of Stallings' dirt came to light. They wanted this shit resolved and quickly. They wanted Stallings dead.

I almost lost my high when Mrs. Bullock told us there was five hundred grand waiting on us if we would take the job. She said she would give us fifty thousand to start and the balance for his head. There was no way we could turn it down. No fuckin' way.

We stayed with Mrs. Bullock until ten that morning. She went out to pick up our money. She told us that she'd rather go get it than getting us mixed up with the powers that be. Her rationale suited us just fine. I didn't want to know any of the mothafuckas calling shots like these. I was sure by now they knew who I was, but I wasn't interested in their asses—not one bit. "*What a nigga didn't see, he didn't know*," was my philosophy behind the shit. When she came back, she had all the money in cash.

"But we need a car, Mrs. Bullock. I'm sure Stallings already knows what we're driving and I think we should change up on him just in case."

She said, "Follow me."

We went with Mrs. Bullock to the back of her estate. She led us down an unpaved driveway into a wooden garage that looked like it had been around much longer than she'd been living. She opened it and sitting before our eyes was a black nineteen-eighty El Camino with only fifty miles on it.

"Oh, my damn," Rossi said.

"It's in mint condition." I was in love.

Mrs. Bullock ran her hand across the hood. "It was my husband's. He never drove it after he bought it. I guess he was too busy being chauffeured around everywhere. Use this. I'm sure it can get you where you need to go."

split the fifty grand with Rossi. When I got back home I whipped out my half in front of Lauren, put five grand in her hand, and told Lauren to go to the mall and get her wardrobe together. Finally my luck was changing. I didn't tell Lauren where the money had come from. She had been through enough. She prodded but I wasn't telling. If I had, it would have made her think about not being able to have children because of what Stallings had done to her by his lynch men.

When the girls left, we went to work. I tuned the car up and Rossi helped me to wash it. We changed our clothes and began to roll in the streets. We didn't know where to find Stallings, besides down at the station, and there was no way I was going to smoke his ass there. Mrs. Bullock gave us his address but knew just like we did that the hard-on had too much ruthless shit going on in his life to be sitting at home. But we still took a chance to check his place and sat in front of his house in College Park. We sat for nearly three hours without any sign of him. Then Rossi had an idea.

"Remember the young boy that Stallings had slinging dope for him?"

"Yeah?"

"He'll know where to find him."

"You think?"

"Trust me. If you're handling narcotics for a mothafucka, you know where he's at, at all times."

I had to call Mrs. Bullock to get the info on this young cat. Her contacts didn't have an address for him, but she told me he had moved locations and most of his time was now spent downtown, selling coke and crack to the corporate types working in the high-rises and wearing the best of suits. We hit the streets and began looking for him.

I let Rossi take the lead because he was really good with talking with these street thugs. It was in his blood. He even seemed to be enjoying himself, mixing it up with those who only had one thing on their minds: getting high or paid. After a few hours we had the general area and corner that Julian a.k.a. "Sweetness" worked, and we stood near a MARTA bus stop until we finally saw him around midnight. Rossi approached him.

"Yo, yo, what's up?"

"What the fuck you mean whas' up, white boy? You either want to get some of this good shit or you want to get the fuck outtta my face," Sweetness said. Sweetness was about five-eight, one-fifty pounds, light-skinned with a short haircut. He was wearing brand-new jeans and fresh sneakers.

"Young boy, it ain't gotta be like that," Rossi told him.

He snapped. "Well, that's exactly how it is."

"Look, I need some information," Rossi said.

"What the fuck I look like—the asshole that works in the info booth or some shit? Get outta my face."

I moved in on the young boy. "Look, little nigga. You need to shut the fuck up and listen."

He looked around at us. "Oh, what's this shit?"

"It's exactly what it looks like. Two old players on your young ass if you don't shut up and listen."

"What?"

"You heard him. Do you know a Captain Stallings?" Rossi wanted to know.

"Oh, hell no. I don't know nobody."

"Yes, you do. The police officer who kicked your teeth in and had his men rape your girl," I said.

The young nigga paused.

Rossi told him. "Yeah, you know him. You're out here slinging dope for him, too, ain't you? That was some fucked-up shit he did to you and your girl. I bet you still slinging for him, ain't you?"

"So, what of it?"

"So what he did was wrong," I told him.

"And we know you want to see him pay," Rossi added.

Sweetness began to walk away. "Look, I ain't got shit to say."

We began to walk right beside him. Rossi on the left, I was on his right. "Fine, be his bitch for the rest of your life," I told him.

"That's right. It won't be long until your girl realizes you ain't nothing but a bitch working for somebody else anyway," Rossi pushed.

Sweetness stopped walking. "Man, why the fuck are ya'll stressing me?"

"We need information," I told him.

"About what?"

Rossi said, "Where we can find Stallings, that's all."

"And why in the fuck should I tell you?"

Rossi pulled out a thousand dollars and put it in his face. "Because you should. Here, take it. It's more money than he's ever given you." Sweetness looked at the money, then at both of us. "Go 'head, take it," Rossi prodded. When Sweetness reached for the money, Rossi pulled back. "Where can we find him?"

➤ ➤ ➤

Sweetness told us that Stallings had a hideaway up in Buckhead. It was a townhouse that no one else knew about except for his cronies and some of the young bucks he had selling for him. Sweetness told us that many of the Atlanta Hawks stayed in the complex during the season and Stallings loved living there because he was a die-hard basketball fan who couldn't get enough of professional basketball players. The complex was a sight to see, and I realized Stallings must have been pushing a lot of weight to be able to afford such a place.

I'd planned to go into Stallings' place, take care of business and leave him lying, dripping in his own blood for the coroner to come pick him up. It was late, so I was sure he was asleep—at least the guard at the entrance of the community seemed to be. We turned off the car lights and slipped right past him.

I told Rossi that I would go in first and for him to wait ten minutes before coming inside. Stallings had too much confidence in his community's security because his sliding-glass door leading to his bedroom off the patio was wide open, so I slid open the door and let myself in. As soon as I took one step in his bedroom, I felt a cold piece of steel damn near take my face off. Then the lights were turned on.

"Well, well. Look at this," Stallings said as he walked out of his bathroom after the guy who hit me in the face told him it was all clear. He told the punk holding me at bay, "Remind me to thank that bitch, Sweetness, will you?" The ugly asshole who hit me was rubbing his hand. I think the recoil of the steel had pained his hand. He nodded his head, then smiled and showed me every bit of his yuck mouth, which was missing at least four teeth up front.

"I don't believe you have the audacity to break into my place, nigga," Stallings said to me.

"Look, I don't..." His thug hit me in the mouth again.

"I don't have time for this punk ass nigga, Deion. I don't care what he has to say; I want you to take him to his car. Follow us out on Moreland and when our deal is finished, we're going to kill him."

The thug sounded like he had a third-grade education, and he smelled like a fifth of liquor. "You gonna let me do this one, boss?"

Stallings just smiled.

Stallings' thug walked me out to the car. All I could think about was which way I was going to fall to the ground once Rossi saw me coming out with a busted eye and in front of this big ass punk who was twisting the shit out of my arm. I led him to the car but when we got there, Rossi wasn't. I looked around hoping that he would jump out the bushes and start capping but it never happened. Asshole pushed me in the El Camino and we sped off following Stallings.

We must have ridden in the car a good twenty minutes. For the life of me, I couldn't figure out what the fuck happened to Rossi. I thought maybe he went inside to see if I needed help while I was on the way out. Whatever happened to him, I kind of figured I was fucked.

Stallings pulled into one of the many distribution centers that shipped truck parts on Moreland Avenue. This one had a bunch of rigs on the lot. We parked in between them and I could see the Starlight Drive-In Movie Theater from a distance. Deion pulled me out the car, hit me in the back of the head and stood me up straight as another car pulled up shortly afterwards.

"Well, at least you get to see how a drug deal goes down before you die," Stallings sneered at me. "Don't say a word or I'll have you shot on the spot."

When the black sedan came to a complete stop, I recognized the scrawny bastard who got out. It was DA Anderson. He looked at me. "What the hell is this, Stallings?"

"Just some business I need to take care of when we're finished here," Stallings told him. "You got my product?"

"Yes, I have it. That's why I'm here."

"Let me see," Stallings instructed.

Anderson moved closer to me. "Wait a minute, wait a minute. Where do I know you from?"

I didn't answer.

"He's the jack-off on that Pete Rossi case, one of the jurors. He cut a deal with Rossi to get his ass off for a cut of the money he stole from us. But I got it back and now I have to teach him a lesson when we finish here."

Anderson's punk ass shook his head in disgust, spit in my face and then slapped me. The little bitch hit like a lady but I played as though it hurt. "Next time, stay out of grown men's business," he told me.

"Okay, damn it. Show me the narcotic," Stallings said.

"You got my money?" Anderson wanted to know.

Stallings pointed at a briefcase on the ground next to his feet. "It's all there."

"I thought I was scandalous," I told them and then Deoin hit me across the face with a wicked forehand.

Anderson showed Stallings the drugs. Stallings smiled and Deoin reached out for Anderson's briefcase and put it securely under his arm. Anderson bent down to pick up his money and when he touched the briefcase, Stallings pulled out his pistol and shot him in the head and chuckled when he fell backwards. He startled Deoin and me.

"Damn!" Deoin screamed. "Now that's what I call a business deal."

Stallings turned to Deoin. "That was powerful, wasn't it?"

"Sure the hell was. Hey, I bet you I'll make this one drop faster," Deoin said. Then he pulled his pistol and pointed it at my head. At that moment I knew that God probably didn't want to hear a word from me, after all the shit I'd done over the last couple of months, so I just closed my eyes and got myself ready to explain. I heard Deoin cock back his pistol and as soon as he told me to say goodnight, the covered hatch of the El Camino was flipped open.

"No, you say good night, mothafuckas!" Rossi screamed. Rossi surprised them so much that they barely had time to get off a few rounds in response. In a matter of seconds they were both lying on the ground next to Anderson. I was in shock and lay on the ground still, praying that my black ass wasn't shot.

"Yo? Yo? West? You all right? "Rossi wanted to know.

"My...mothafuckin' nigga...my-motha-fuckin-nigga" was all I could say after we made sure I didn't have any holes in my body and Rossi pulled me from off the ground.

43

The very next day Mrs. Bullock called and told us she was on her way over. It wasn't a surprise to me that the day was sunny without a cloud in the sky. Earlier that morning Lauren personally saw Lex to the bus station on her way back to North Carolina to start anew. We hadn't slept much that night because Rita and Lauren wanted to talk about what they were going to do with their share of the money and hear what happened to us over and over again. Plus, there was a decision to make about the money and blow left in the two briefcases from Anderson and Stallings' drug deal. There was no way we were leaving any of it there. Rossi chose to hold on to the drugs. He didn't tell me what he had planned and, at that point, I didn't want to know. I chose the money, so it was an even exchange.

Rossi was with me in the garage while I washed up the El Camino. I wanted to have it in top shape when Mrs. Bullock arrived. I even thought about asking her to buy the car since it brought me so much good luck. When she arrived we had just finished waxing the car and were enjoying a couple of brews while a group of kids down the street played hard in a game of pick-up basketball. Others were screaming at the top of their lungs playing kickball in the street. Dunkin had finally made his way over to my shop like I told him after I stopped him from jumping on Lauren at the drive-in. I had him take a break from cleaning the oil off my shop floor and told him to go down the street and open up a fire hydrant for the youngsters.

"Sure is nice out here today, boys," Mrs. Bullock said.

"Sure is."

"That it is," Rossi assured right before he took another gulp of his brew.

"Well, the money has been deposited into each of your accounts and here are your deposit slips."

"Oh, my damn," Rossi said as soon as his eyes focused on the amount.

Mrs. Shirley Bullock had a very sincere look on her face. "I want you boys to know, I didn't enjoy being a part of what happened," she said. "But my late husband always used to tell me, 'Sometimes things have to happen for others to keep moving forward in a positive manner.' I think in the long run, my decision about being a part of this will serve me right. I think I'll be able to live with it, because remember it wasn't about you or me. It was about this great city and not letting it fall victim to scum."

"We understand."

"We sure do. No need to explain to me. I'm with you," Rossi assured.

"You know, I was thinking," Mrs. Bullock said. "You two make a pretty good team. Maybe you should think about being private detectives?"

I looked at Rossi. "No disrespect, Mrs. Bullock—but hell no."

Rossi said. "Yeah, yeah. He's right—don't have the stomach for it," he explained.

Lauren joined us all and I put my arm around her.

"You sure are a pretty black girl," Mrs. Bullock said.

"Why, thank you!" Lauren said.

After shooting us a heartfelt conquering smile, Mrs. Bullock looked down the street at the kids playing under the sun. There was no doubt in my mind that what she had been a part of was especially done for them. She gave us another glancing over and began toward her car, no doubt on her way home to sit in her mansion all by her lonesome. "Now you stay out of trouble, you hear?"

"Sure will," Rossi answered.

"Without a doubt," I told her. When she was halfway to her car, I called out to her. "Mrs. Bullock? I…I was wonder'n if you wanted to sell this here car to me? You know, it's my good-luck charm now. But, if not, I'll bring it right out to you."

She smiled back at me. "Child, you go 'head and keep that car. Just take good care of it, okay?"

Lauren kissed me on the cheek and Rossi patted me on the back.

"I sure will, Mrs. Bullock. And thank you, and I really do mean that."

Rossi ran up to open the car door for her and shut it when she was settled. She called out, "You're quite welcome, son, and I'll see you in a couple of days to get mine washed. You'll still be open for business, right?" she asked through her window, right after she cranked her car.

Mrs. Bullock began to drive away. I yelled out to her, "Oh, yeah, you don't have to worry about that, Mrs. Bullock. We're about to get things crack'n around here. And don't you worry about paying either. You never have to pay here again...Never again."

ABOUT THE AUTHOR

Franklin White is the author of the national bestsellers
Fed Up with the Fanny, Cup of Love and *'Til Death Do Us Part,*
a short story collection nominated for a Gold Pen Award.
Money For Good is Franklin's third novel. His next novel,
Potentially Yours, will be released in June 2004. He is the
former features editor for *Upscale* magazine as well as the writer
of the column "Author2Author." He is an inductee of the Archie
Givens Collection at the University Of Minnesota. Franklin White
is also publisher of Blue/Black Press and has worked on such
notable titles as *No Matter What* with Bridgett Stewart,
the soon to be released *Tamara Jones: The Last Good Kiss*
by Janice Pinnock, and *Playing With the Hand I Was
Dealt* by Nikki Jenkins.
Visit www.franklin-white.com.

Printed in the United States
By Bookmasters